# BABCHI

---

A LOVE STORY

V BRAY

Babchi: A Love Story
Copyright © 2021 by V Bray



Babchi: A Love Story ISBN 978-1-7362599-1-7 (paperback)

*To my beloved Anna, always.*

1

___________

## KATIE

**Suburban New Jersey**

Katie lifts open the living room window by her grandmother; Babchi's lifeless body is still warm on the rented hospital bed. Her mother, the ever-practical scientist, is in the front yard greeting the police and undertaker, shamelessly efficient in dealing with her mother's passing. Katie's brother and sister left a week ago, too busy with non-stop work to wait for death's slow pace. But the library where Katie works gave her a week to stay with Babchi through the process of each organ shutting down while hospice administered morphine and painkillers. Hopefully, Babchi was unaware of any pain.

Katie feels a tear slide down her cheek, and she pushes back her short, straight hair. The winter sun shines harshly through the bay window. Christmas came and went amidst the blur of ambulance rides, hospital visits, and faked joviality. Now on New Year's Eve, Katie imagines Babchi's spirit, the spirit that was Katie's rock, lifting up out of the body that housed it. Katie places a hand first on each of the arms that held and comforted her through her moody twenties, then on the lips that kissed every childhood hurt away, and last over the eyelids covering the blue-gray eyes that lit up whenever Katie visited. She reaches over the prone body and pushes the small side window wider, allowing the dry air in. Holding Babchi's familiar wrinkled hand, she whispers, "Goodbye." Another tear falls. She pictures Babchi's spirit free, released out the window.

Ambulance workers bustle in, and Katie moves aside, watching in awe and horror as her mother almost happily directs the scene: in-charge, in command, director of the show.

"Well, we knew it was coming." Katie's mother shakes her head at the EMS crew as they produce yet another form for her to sign. Even in death, there is endless paperwork. Katie's mother grabs a pen off the cluttered side table and scribbles furiously, indenting each page with her signature.

No one notices Katie as she wanders past the body and the old bed that has held so much suffering. Katie wonders what else the EMS can do. Babchi is gone. Shouldn't hospice be here by now? She glances out the hall window and watches the flashing lights coming from the four police cars out front. In this small town, death is big news. Considering it is New Year's Eve, it is unlikely anyone is too thrilled to be on duty.

*It figures Babchi chose to make her death as unforgettable an event as possible,* Katie thinks, managing a lopsided smile. Babchi had a flair for the dramatic.

Katie walks into the tiny bathroom off the hall and shuts the door. She sits on the edge of the tub, her knees banging up against the toilet. She takes in a deep, shuddering breath, filling her nostrils with the clean smell of bleach. Katie washed the room thoroughly right before Babchi started hospice care. It has only been seven days. The hyper-efficiency of the cancer was unreal. Head in her hands, Katie isn't ready to cry. Not here, not in front of these people.

"No, I don't want to."

Katie hears her aunt's voice carry from behind the bedroom door across the hall. The small Cape Cod only has one floor, two bedrooms, and no insulation. It is safe and snug, and in the winter Babchi used to close all the interior doors and live solely in the front room where she set the thermostat to a balmy eighty degrees.

"Hanna, are you sure you wouldn't like to say goodbye?" Katie's mother calls down the hall to the bedroom.

"Karolina, stop. I'm not one of your patients. I'll come out once they've taken her away," a muffled voice carries back.

"I still think it would be best if you came out," Katie's mother says, unwilling to give in. "In order to grieve properly, one must see the body."

"Ugh, stop it," Hanna calls back to her sister, still behind the closed door. "Just because you're a doctor..." Katie tunes out the voices as streams of memory flood her mind: Babchi hugging her, holding her, explaining how and why Katie should give her mother one more chance. And Katie always did—for Babchi. Katie wipes an errant tear away. For years, she forgave her mother's judgments and criticisms that all stemmed from the fact that Katie isn't like them; she is a librarian in a family of brilliant doctors and one lawyer, her brother.

Katie shudders. *He'll be here soon,* she thinks. She and her brother haven't spoken since Babchi's diagnosis. Only three months ago, she was in the hospital room as her mother—in full surgeon regalia—explained to Babchi that there was no point in further testing or biopsies. Babchi had pancreatic cancer, practically a death sentence. Through those months since the diagnosis, Katie clung to the hope that Babchi would take charge of her last days.

But, sadly, Babchi didn't argue. Instead, she let Katie's mom set up hospice care while Katie's brother drew up the paperwork; then Babchi signed her life away blindly. There was no resistance left in the woman who had fought to survive almost all her life.

More tears fall. *Not now,* Katie scolds herself. *You can't let them see. It's weakness.* Katie knows that in a room full of apex predators, you do not show weakness.

She stands up and pats her cheeks dry, checking her reflection in the small vanity mirror. Pointed chin, large brown eyes—*a kitten face,* she hears Babchi's smiling voice say. *Maybe this is how it will be now,* she thinks. *Ghost whispers of memories and voices rising unbidden.* Katie leans in closer to the mirror and strains to hear Babchi's heavily accented voice call her, *Kitten, my angel, kotek. I am sorry.*

"You in there, Katie?"

Katie's head snaps up. It's her sister. After swiftly wiping her eyes one more time, Katie opens the door.

"Oh, Katie." Ada hugs Katie and steps back. She is as impeccable as ever in slim jeans and a black knit sweater. She is five years Katie's senior and close to forty; most people think they are twins. "You ready to work?" Ada holds up a bucket of cleaning supplies.

"They haven't even taken her," Katie whispers fiercely. "And Aunt Hanna is holed up in Babchi's bedroom."

Ada smiles. "She's still afraid of dead bodies?"

Katies shakes her head. Of course, Ada doesn't understand or even respect their aunt's fear. A surgeon like their mother, Ada spends her days rewiring nerves. Her Christmas announcement was that she received a job offer to be part of a groundbreaking neuro-regeneration team at a large research hospital.

"Don't worry. I'll get her out of there." Ignoring Katie's horrified look, Ada turns, pushes past their mother, and opens the bedroom door.

"Ada, get out!" Aunt Hanna's sharp voice fills the house, but everyone knows it's near impossible to win against Ada. The bedroom door clicks closed behind her.

Katie walks away from the heated debate echoing down the hall and back into the front room as the hospice doctor declares Babchi truly dead. The EMS team heave Babchi's body off the rented bed and place her in a black bag, so well-known from TV crime shows. Katie turns away. It's too final. She hears the zipper close, the squeak of stretcher wheels, and grunts of exertion as the men carry her grandmother's heavy body down the front steps.

The screen door closes, and Ada bustles out of the bedroom and announces, "Well, I'm going to start in here." Her face is tight, unused to losing an argument. Aunt Hanna is still in the bedroom.

Ada walks between piles of old newspapers and Polish magazines to the rented hospital bed beside the front bay window. They thought Babchi would enjoy looking out into her garden, in which she spent so much time.

"This carpet will have to go." Ada runs a foot over the stained, yellow, wall-to-wall carpet. "Well, at least there aren't that many rooms to clean up." She starts to strip the hospital bed. "What do you want to tackle, Katie?"

Katie takes in the bottles of pain meds on the dusty side table, the sagging sofa where Babchi consoled Katie after every breakup, and the piles of papers and boxes laying in the corners. Babchi said she would clean up "her papers" and get them in order, but it never happened. *Doesn't matter much now,* Katie thinks.

On cue, the screen door opens, and Matt walks in. He's wearing tailored jeans, Italian leather shoes, and a blazer—the casual look of a lawyer.

"Already cleaning up the hoarding, I see." He smiles and kisses Ada on the cheek. She leans into him in a half-hug.

*Two peas in a pod,* Katie thinks, remembering back to when they were kids. All she can picture are her two siblings' backs; she can almost feel the pounding of her feet as she endlessly chased after them. *I never caught up.* Katie braces herself as her brother walks over.

"Poor Katie," her brother says and embraces her in a hug. "This must be difficult for you." He pulls back and searches Katie's expression, false concern etched into every line of his handsome face.

"Thanks, Matt." Katie pulls out of the awkward embrace. His voice alone brings back a lifetime of cruel judgments and barbed comments always delivered in an ever-so-reasonable tone.

"So, how's the job? Are you going to be able to make rent without Babchi?" Her brother cuts right to the chase.

Katie's cheeks blush red. Ada turns away, already wiping down the plastic-enclosed mattress with disinfectant. Katie is in disbelief that nothing has changed between them, and yet...

"I don't want to do this," Katie says. With a final glance at the spot where Babchi had lain bedridden, Katie walks out of the house.

2

———

**ANNA**

**Poland, Spring 1940**

"Anna, come help your father," Anna's mother calls, her voice carrying from the kitchen area up to the loft.

"It's fine, fine." Anna's father shoos Anna away as she steps down the ladder from the loft and rushes over to him. Despite his dismissal, Anna scoops up his mud-covered boots and begins wiping them down with a rag.

He sits, his eyes sparkling in the lamplight. "Did you find the mushrooms, Ania?"

Anna smiles. At seventeen, she is training to become a forester like her father. An employee of the Polish Parks Department, her father holds a small government job as caretaker of the forest that borders Lithuania, and near the Soviet Union. He is teaching Anna everything about the dark fir forest they call home, hoping one day his independent daughter will find a forest of her own to care for.

"Yes, Papa." From her skirt pocket Anna draws a perfect

cream globe with light flaking on the edges. Anna delights in learning the medicinal properties of all the flora found in the forest. If her identification is correct, this is a prize among medicinal mushrooms.

"Ahh." Her father reaches out a hand to inspect her choice. "Very good, Ania." She beams under his praise.

"Enough, then." Anna's mother cuts them off. "It's time to get the food on the table. We don't want to fall asleep in our soup." Anna's mother's voice softens at the end. A city woman born and educated in Vilnius, she cannot understand her daughter's love of the forest.

"You heard your mother. I'm famished." Anna's father stands and heads over to the wash basin with Anna. "You did very well today," he whispers in her ear. Anna smiles and leans her head against his shoulder.

The family gathers around the rough-hewn fir table. Her father sits at the head of the table and her mother at the foot, with the twin six-year-old boys between them on one side and the three girls on the other side. Tadek, the eldest son, is studying law at Krakow University.

"Any word from the town?" Anna's mother asks. During his rounds through the forest, Anna's father often meets town families picking mushrooms or berries. Kindly, he turns a blind eye to the minor theft and uses the opportunity to gather information.

Anna's father's brow creases. "Nothing about Tadek." He hopes his son is staying out of the political turmoil. A year ago, Poland had been annexed, half to Germany and half to the USSR. Hopefully, in the forest, they will be safe.

"Any other news?" asks Beata, the eldest daughter. Most like their petite mother, Beata is their mother's right hand, much like Anna is her father's.

"No," their father answers and turns to the boys, "but the Stanislaw brothers got a new wind-up train from their father." The boys' eyes grow wide. Their friend's father is the local banker, so his children always have the latest toys. "I spoke to their father a few days ago. He invited you to come by and play with them next time we go to town."

"What color is it?" "Does it have a caboose?" "How many cars?" The boys throw questions at their father while the family finishes their supper of game stew and freshly baked bread. Five new loaves sit cooling by the cast iron oven. It is baking day.

WARM AND FULLY FED, Anna helps her mother tuck the younger children into bed before settling down for her daily forestry lesson. She is eager to find out what her next challenge will be. She already excelled in mushroom and wild herb identification. Envious of her father's tracking skills, she hopes he will teach her. He could track anything: man, animal, bird. Anna knows her skills are raw and unformed. She plaits her hair and settles her younger sister Magda into the big bed they share in the loft.

"Did you find the magic mushrooms?" Magda whispers.

Anna laughs softly so as not to wake the twins sleeping one bed over. "Yes, I did."

Magda's eyes sparkle. "When can we go to the city?"

Anna smiles gently at her sister. Magda, six years her junior, yearns for society and the arts; she feels the pull of the city. Anna enjoys visiting the large cities sometimes, but like her father, she prefers the solitude of the forest. Their tiny cottage is perfect in her eyes. She can't imagine living like her mother's family—hemmed in by buildings on either side.

"Maybe this weekend. But do not get your hopes up, Magda. Grandmother is old." Anna has been helping her father care for his aging mother-in-law. The medicinal properties of the mushroom she found today will help their grandmother's pain, but Anna doesn't have the heart to tell Magda that there is no cure, or that death is unstoppable.

Magda nods and closes her eyes. Anna kisses the girl on the forehead and climbs down the ladder to the big room to sit with her father.

"I hear rumors, Bogdan." Anna's mother is wiping down the table and talking softly to her husband.

"It is nothing, dear." Anna's father shakes his head. "We are safe here in the forest. They will not bother us."

Anna's stomach knots up. She heard rumors of advancing forces, but being so far away in the countryside makes it hard to distinguish what is true. She quickly quells the fear she feels rising and looks out the window into the shadowy night. Father is right. Whatever trouble happens in the towns or the cities will not affect them here.

"Papa, ready for my lesson?" Anna asks and steps forward as if she hasn't been eavesdropping.

Anna's father looks up at her tiredly. "Not tonight. It was a long day, and spring has only just started." He ruffles her wavy brown hair. "Tomorrow. I promise."

Anna sighs, disappointment clear on her face. She kisses both her mother and father goodnight, then climbs back up to the bedroom.

"Why so early to bed? Did you fail the mushroom test?"

"Maybe I put all the bad mushrooms into your soup fixings!" Anna teases as she turns to her older sister and slides into the small cot Beata has all to herself. Only two years older than Anna, they are best friends.

Beata chuckles quietly. "Then we'll all be running around the house seeing things! Maybe chipmunks will do our laundry, clean..."

They both giggle while remembering the time a small inedible mushroom somehow got into the soup. Luckily, they only suffered slight hallucinations. Beata has no interest in the forest, only cooking. But that incident prompted her to learn the basics of mushroom identification.

"Anna, Mother is worried," Beata says, suddenly serious. Of all the children, she is closest to their mother—their beautiful mother who gave up all modern comforts of city life for love of their father. The girls both know the story by heart, as well as the sacrifices.

"She's always worried about something," Anna says, trying not to be annoyed.

"What if the Germans come? There is so much talk. And the land here is fertile, good game—"

"Stop. It's not time to worry. I can't have you turning into Mother," Anna chides. "I heard them talking. Father doesn't think it will amount to much."

"I hope he's right. But you know he always assumes the best."

"Yes, and Mother the worst. So maybe between them both it will even out." Anna smiles in the dark, happy with her comforting logic. "Goodnight." She turns away and closes her eyes.

Beata gives her a nudge.

"Yes, yes," Anna says and climbs back into the larger bed with Magda.

~

A FEW HOURS LATER, in the dark hours of the morning, Anna hears the faint rumble of an engine. The cranking and popping noises stop somewhere in the clearing in front of the house. Doors slam, and voices are raised. The sun has barely risen.

"Open up!" a man calls while his fists bang on the door.

Anna wakes up cold, a light sweat shining on her forehead. Russian voices. Swiftly, she jumps out of bed and throws on her dress skirts. She nudges Beata awake as she hears her father open the front door.

"What—" she hears her father start to say, but he's cut off by a loud crash.

The twins wake up wide-eyed. Anna hushes them, instructs her sisters to help them get dressed, and rushes down the loft's ladder.

"You, stop." A Russian is in their house. He points a gun at Anna.

She freezes on the last rung. Her father lays sprawled facedown next to the great room's table while her mother stands pale-faced near the kitchen counter. It is still full of freshly baked bread.

The soldier lowers his gun and walks to Anna. He pulls up her face by the chin to force her to look directly into his eyes.

"Go get your siblings. This," he sweeps his hand through the room, "is now the property of the Soviet Union." He pauses and steps back. "And so are you."

"Anna," her father says, standing up slowly. His forehead is bleeding. "Go get your brothers and sisters."

Anna glances at her mother frozen in the kitchen and

notes the two soldiers guarding the door with two more rummaging through cabinets. Shivering, Anna heads back up the ladder and helps her sisters dress the younger children.

**3**

———

**KATIE**

"What do you want to do?" Carly peers into Katie's face, then sits back and waits. She scoops her long red hair into a ponytail.

Katie shakes her head, her face streaked with dried tears. Never mind what she *wants* to do—what *can* she do? Babchi is dead.

"You've been sitting here all week, which I guess is okay with work because it's quiet after the holiday break and all...." Carly's voice trails off as she moves into the kitchen to finish packing her lunch for the day. As a kindergarten teacher in a small private school, Carly is expected to eat with the children at noon. It's good role modeling.

"So, how's our broken bird?" a rough but kind voice asks. Sam, Katie's other roommate, puts her hands on Katie's shoulders. "You going back to work this week?" As an RN, Sam is the quintessential balance of compassion and tough love. Petite, with curly brown hair and bright blue eyes, she has surprised many a difficult patient with her determination.

"I know, I know." Katie returns Sam's inquisitive gaze.

"Monday. I'll go back Monday." The thought wrings the knots tighter in Katie's stomach. How can the world go on? Babchi is dead.

"Well, since it's already Thursday..." Sam shakes her head.

"So, what'd you pack to showcase for the children today?" Katie switches topics and turns to Carly.

"California roll." Carly smiles and goes to the front door to put on her coat. "We have two new Japanese students, and they bring in the most beautiful lunches. Even the simple onigiri—you know, the seaweed-wrapped rice ball—has a plum cut into a star shape as a surprise in the middle! But Michiko's mom makes them herself." She pulls a prepackaged rice ball from her bag.

"Not quite the homemaker yourself?" Sam smirks. She walks to the front door carrying her morning smoothie.

"Well, at least I don't only eat fast food."

Sam's eyes widen, and she shakes the smoothie in Carly's face. "I get points for the one healthy food I get into my system! I know what I'm doing."

"Clogging up your arteries and becoming poised for hypertension?" Carly pushes Sam out of her way and reaches for the door.

"I know the risks. I'm informed." Sam takes a sip of the smoothie. "And with one of these in my body, I can enjoy coffee and cream, no guilt."

"Please, no competitions today!" Katie clutches her head. "You both have stressful jobs, and you combat that in different ways..." Katie trails off, exhausted.

"I just don't get how you stay so healthy." Carly is on a roll. "You work in a hospital, you go out to bars every weekend, and you even smoke sometimes!"

"Good genes?" Sam suggests, taking another swig of her smoothie, this time with a slight grimace.

Cary laughs and turns the door handle. "Carpool is leaving." She shakes her keys in Sam's face.

"All set." Sam is bundled in a heavy parka, earmuffs, and gloves.

Katie silently thanks the universe as they leave. Their banter is hard on her ears and brings back too many memories. She can almost hear Babchi laughing beside her. Katie's grandmother thought Carly and Sam were hilarious. Whenever Babchi visited for Sunday dinner, Carly would entertain everyone with stories of her students' antics, and Sam's drunken bar crawl escapades were the highlight of Babchi's week.

"Better not go back to bed, Katie-girl." Sam holds out a warning finger, the door closing behind her.

"Won't even think of it." Katie smiles.

*Finally, peace.* Katie sighs and curls into the sofa. Babchi's voice echoes through the room: *I'll have enough time to rest when I'm dead.* She always said that when Katie suggested slowing down. *Is she resting now?* Katie wonders. She shuts her eyes tight, and images of Babchi swirl before her closed eyelids. She sees her sitting at the last Christmas before they knew about the cancer. Smiling with a wine glass in hand, she reached out for Katie and pulled her close.

"For my angel," Babchi whispered in Katie's ear as she handed her a small box.

Katie carefully lifted the top and saw a gold ring: one diamond in the middle with chips on either side.

"Your engagement ring?" Katie asked. "I...." She had been dating Liam for six months, but Babchi knew it wasn't going anywhere. There were no secrets between them.

"Darling. I do not expect you to marry that man." Babchi

chuckled. "The ring is not worth much. You know the middle stone is not real. Your grandfather could only afford the chips." She pushed the ring closer to Katie. "You give to your daughter."

Katie felt such mixed emotions. Would she ever have a child?

"Thank you," Katie said and leaned in to hug and kiss her grandmother.

"Well, we hope that you meet a nice man. And then you give me great-grandchildren!" Babchi's eyes twinkled. She loved babies.

"Yeah, yeah." Katie patted Babchi on the back and strung the ring on the gold chain around her neck.

"Go with Sam to a bar, meet a man. You do not need him for more than a night."

"Babchi!" Katie was shocked and amused that her old grandmother was suggesting having a child out of wedlock.

"You do not need a man. But a baby. Imagine a little Katie." Babchi sat back, nodding approvingly at her scheme.

Katie shuddered. "No, thank you. I think one of me is enough."

"My darling, you will regret. And I am an old woman. You want to make me happy, yes?" Babchi's blue-gray eyes searched Katie's.

"Of course, but what would your daughter say?"

"Meh. Karolina will never be happy."

Katie nodded. "So true."

The memory fades away, and Katie wills herself into a dreamless sleep.

# 4

## ANNA

"Hurry, hurry." Anna's mother shoves a loaf of bread into each of the girl's aprons and knots them closed.

Magda watches wide-eyed as the soldiers grow impatient and ram their guns into their father's back. The gash on his head is still seeping blood as he hastens to bundle the twins in warm clothes.

"Enough." The head soldier walks in, a cigarette burning in his hand. Two soldiers gesture to the girls with their guns and motion towards the door. It's time to go.

The early spring air is cold, and the family leaves little puffs of breath trailing behind them. Lotka, the family shepherd, sits by her doghouse waiting expectantly to be called to accompany them.

"Lottie," Magda calls out and runs to the dog.

Anna's mother gasps as the young girl hugs the dog with all her might. The soldiers are shouting, their guns poised. Anna rushes to Magda while her mother shouts in Russian, "Wait, please wait." Anna pulls her sister away.

Magda starts to cry. "But she won't know where we've

gone. She'll be all alone!" The young girl sobs into Anna's shoulder until Anna passes her over to Beata. Then Anna hoists herself into the back of the pickup truck and pulls Magda onto her lap. Beata sits shoulder to shoulder with their mother, gently stroking her hair. Their mother has a strange glassed-over look in her eyes. The soldiers glare at the family as they shut the back of the truck and assume their guard.

The truck puffs smoke into the air and starts to pull away, rattling loudly.

Lottie runs after the truck barking to catch up with the family.

"It's okay, Lottie. Stay, good girl," Beata calls out, biting back tears. She will not let the soldiers see her cry.

Anna tucks Magda's head farther into her shoulder, silently willing their beloved Lottie to turn back.

In a swift movement, one of the soldiers lifts his gun and shoots Lottie mid-run. Beata stifles a scream as Anna forcibly holds Magda's head down.

The soldier sneers at Anna and points at the sobbing young girl. Anna understands the threat.

"Shh, shhh, *moja kochana*, it's time to stop crying," Anna says, knowing there's no room for grief; there is only survival.

5
___________

## KATIE

Katie stretches out on the sofa, willing her mind to relax while the incessant chatter of an old *Gilmore Girls* rerun plays in the background. Throughout Katie's teen years, Babchi would housesit whenever Katie's parents were away at a conference or vacationing. Memories begin to swirl through Katie's mind.

"No, Katie. It is dream. A young mother cleaning? She cannot afford that house and those clothes!"

"But she's the manager of an inn, Babchi. My problem is with how much food they eat. They would be so fat." Katie enjoyed getting her grandmother fired up.

"Yes, yes," Babchi agreed. "Skinny people do not eat. Only way to lose weight is stop eating." Babchi shook her head and laughed. "I tried every diet. So young and stupid. Even the grapefruit diet. Only grapefruit!"

"Very silly," Katie agreed and leaned into Babchi's shoulder.

"What do you want for dinner? Apple pancakes?" Babchi asked, stroking Katie's hair.

"Mmmmm..." Katie nodded and sat up. "More calories

than grapefruit. But can you have that much sugar?" Katie poked Babchi's chubby arm. Katie's mother had mentioned something about pre-diabetes. Anyone could see that at two hundred pounds, Babchi was overweight.

"I'm old woman. What do I care how I look?" She laughed and stood up. "Do not worry, *kochana*."

Katie shuts down the memory and watches as Lorelai breaks up with yet another man, just one in a steady stream of dates and boyfriends. Katie can relate. She remembers her latest fiasco with a software developer. In the end, she found out he was stringing three other women along, telling each of them he was being exclusive. Ridiculous. Men treated internet dating like a shopping experience—*what better deal can I get?* At least it was only three months of bull-shit, Katie reminds herself.

She wanders into the kitchen, the cold winter air chilling the apartment as she reaches to turn on the kettle. Brittle sunlight creeps in through the slatted blinds as Katie pulls out her favorite mug: gaudy red and pink hearts cover it alongside proclamations of love. Another Babchi dollar-store gift. Tears well in her eyes. *You are my sunshine,* Babchi's gravelly singing voice echoes in Katie's mind as she remembers their last Valentine's Day. Babchi knew how to give an over-the-top, heartfelt present.

Katie missed that feeling of total acceptance. Babchi knew Katie was stuck, but unlike her parents and siblings, she didn't blame Katie for her low-paying job at the library. When Katie was promoted to tech supervisor, she was briefly happy until she discovered that along with her new title, she was simply assigned more duties and not more money. *Well, at least it got me off the circulation desk,* she thinks wryly. How many more years could she keep a straight face as patrons argued over a ten-cent fine? The worst were those same patrons she later spotted at the local specialty shop spending hundreds on gourmet food.

She pours the freshly boiled water over a teabag. Babchi drank coffee with cream and lots of sugar. When Katie was a child, Babchi would let her drink some of the sugary drink. Katie smiles fondly, remembering her first coffee and the jolt she felt after drinking the hot liquid. When Katie's mother found out Babchi was sharing her coffee with a child, she let Babchi have it. But Babchi could give it right back. She was the only one who could stand up against Katie's mother. Katie's mother didn't truly care what the pair were up to at home as long as it didn't mess up her perfect house or Katie's perfect older siblings.

Katie slowly carries her tea back to the sofa to settle in for another day. The dull throbbing in her head lessens with every sip of caffeine. Katie puts the mug down and lets her eyes close, drifting into darkness.

6
___

## ANNA

**Traveling East**

Anna's eyes are heavy with exhaustion as the truck bumps along country roads. She envies the younger children who somehow manage to sleep. The truck refills with petrol once, at which point Anna and her family are allowed to relieve themselves. She ushers Magda off the truck and instructs the girl to crouch behind some bushes while she spreads out her skirts for extra cover.

Thankfully, she doesn't have to worry about these soldiers. They have lost interest in the prisoners, so when the girls get back on the truck, Anna's mother is able to slip bread to each of them. Anna's father has been asleep in a crumpled heap at the back of the truck since they were taken. His forehead is swollen, and dirt is crusted over the gash.

Anna sits quietly chewing her chunk of bread, amazed at how resilient the body is. Her father taught her that. The medicines they collected and dispensed to the townspeople all worked on the biological prerogative of a body's will to live. *It is in us,* she muses and bites another piece of bread. And yet... Anna glances at their mother: shaking hands, pale skin, delicate bones. Anna did not inherit any of her mother's refined looks. She rubs her arm, feeling her rough skin. It is perfect for walking through forest brambles without getting scratched. Average height and stocky, Anna has enough weight to stay warm through the forest winters, too. She chews another piece of bread and observes her delicate twin brothers huddled around their mother. High cheekbones, skin brushed pink on white, matching pale blond heads with deep slate-blue eyes that stare groggily back at her. Their eyes are the one familial trait between all her brothers and sisters—eyes that could look as blue as a summer sky then turn instantly into a cloudy storm. They are her mother's eyes.

Anna looks down at Magda. The child's blond curls fan out on Anna's lap. She strokes the fine hair while Magda sleeps. *So young and so vain,* Anna thinks, smiling to herself. Slightly more delicate in build than Anna, at eleven years old Magda spends more hours in front of the small, shared mirror than any of her siblings. She braids her hair intricately over and over until she achieves the desired effect of tendrils framing her face and eyes. Anna pictures her sister's favorite blue dress that they left hanging on the wall of their bedroom. She knows her sister will miss it. The dress made her eyes turn an electric blue, an effect that garnered Magda numerous compliments whenever they went to town. Anna wonders if they will ever have that carefree life again.

"Anna," Beata whispers and settles down next to her sister. "I'm worried about Father."

Their father is silent at the back of the truck. The soldier guarding their exit has dozed off in the twilight. They have been captive for two days.

"Here." Anna slips Magda's head from her lap and places it gently on Beata's. Crouching low to the bed of the truck, she shuffles down the length to her father.

"Papa." He doesn't respond. "Papa," she says again, gently pushing his shoulder while glancing at the soldier.

Her father stirs and opens his eyes; the left one tears up with the effort.

"I want to check your wound before it's dark."

Her father nods. With nimble fingers, Anna first wraps her dirty hand in the clean lining of her coat, then feels around the swelling on his forehead.

"I am not touching the wound," she reassures her father, showing him her carefully wrapped hand. "Only the clean part will touch."

"How is it?" Her father's voice is scratchy and dry.

"It does not look infected," she murmurs. "And there's no heat. Let me look at your eye." Her voice is gentle and firm.

Her father strains to open his swollen eye. Anna blinks to hold back the rush of tears that threaten to spill. Her father pats her hand down away from his wound.

"This will heal, Anna." He holds her gaze with his deep brown eyes. "This," he places her hand over her heart, "this you must work to heal."

Anna nods, almost wishing she were as young as Magda. Then, despite her fear, she could still be comforted simply by the presence of her family.

"Keep your eyes and ears open. And watch your sister."

"But Papa—"

"You must take care of Magda and the twins." He drops her hand. "I do not know where they are taking us. They may not let families stay together." He pulls her in for a hug. "We must be prepared."

Anna squeezes her father, absorbing his strength of will. "Yes, I am." She pulls back and kisses him on the cheek. "I understand."

## 7

## KATIE

Aloud ringing wakes Katie. She presses the "stop" button on her phone alarm and rolls back into the pillows, covering her face with her blanket. Morning light drifts though the small daisy pattern, throwing shadows across her arms. When she was a little girl, her mother would leave her at Babchi's rambling Victorian house on the outskirts of downtown Paterson. Katie had loved the old house, which was partitioned into numerous small rooms and had a winding back staircase that connected all four floors. To her, it was a fairytale house where her time was spent eating savory homecooked meals, going on trips to the bakery, and playing—lots and lots of playing. As a child, she hadn't known the house was falling apart. After Katie's grandfather died, Babchi let Katie's mom handle the sale of the decrepit house so they could move Babchi closer to the family.

The daisy shadows dance on Katie's arms as she remembers. Once, while her mother was completing her residency, Katie was left in Babchi's care for three months. It was spring, but Babchi took out the Christmas decorations and turned the first floor into an enchanted fairyland. They strung red, green, and gold Christmas tree chains that sparkled against the rainbow-colored tree lights. Katie hung snowflake and icicle ornaments from the artificial tree branches. Babchi created a hideaway by draping the dining room chairs in colorful sheets and stringing garland along the edges. To anyone else, it was a child's fort made of sheets and chairs, but to Katie it was a magical palace that extended out the side door where a canopy of purple wisteria bloomed in a long arc along the length of the house. After four weeks of playing in her very own kingdom, Katie's grandfather demanded his dining room back.

Katie sighs and runs a hand over the patterned blanket, disrupting the soft shadows. *Time to go back to work.* Goosebumps rise on her skin. She hears Sam and Carly banging around in the kitchen and knows it's only a matter of time before one or both of them checks in on her.

Can she face the world? Katie would never admit it to anyone, but she can't truly remember what she's done since Babchi died. Has it only been a week? She rubs the sleep and unshed tears from her eyes and prepares to face the day.

WALKING INTO THE SMALL LIBRARY, Katie is relieved to find it empty. *Came early enough,* she thinks, walking quickly through the back-office area to the main part of the building. Two rows of computers for public use glare at her. Glancing over all twenty computers, she sees as least five covered in bright sticky notes. She groans. The oldest computers constantly break down because they can't handle the latest web technology. Katie collects the sticky notes, crumples them in her hand, and reboots the machines. She knows what it feels like, not being able to keep up. *Maybe if I smack a sticky note on me, I'll be retired like these old computers should be,* she jokes to herself. *Or, at least, everyone will leave me alone.*

Katie opens the door to her tiny office, shoves her bag in her desk, and notices two cards tilted upright on her desk. Probably condolence cards. She pushes them aside, clicks on her computer, and opens up her email. *Better get down to it,* she encourages herself, then falls into a rhythm of answer, delete, or save. A few hours pass, and she wonders why no one has come to ask for help. Usually, she's called out to fix a computer problem at least twice an hour. She considers checking out what's going on, but instead she opens her lunch bag and eats the turkey sandwich Carly packed for her that morning. There's so much email and committee work to catch up on.

"Katie? Katie?" a voice is calling.

Katie looks up to see Maggie, the Adult Reference Librarian and her friend, peeking in through the office door.

"Oh, hey." Katie pushes back from her desk.

"It's almost time to go home."

"What?" Katie shakes her head and looks at the clock: three P.M. What happened to her day?

"Computers One and Two are down again. But I put the 'Out of Order' signs on them, so the night crew shouldn't get any complaints." Maggie peers at Katie over her glasses. With short, cropped hair, tortoise-shell glasses, and a cardigan, Maggie is the quintessential librarian.

"Um, okay. Thanks." Katie scrambles to remember details. Did she eat lunch? Does she have to use the bathroom? Should she be worried she doesn't know the answer to any of these questions?

"Well, I'm taking off now. See you tomorrow?"

"Yes, of course. Tomorrow." Katie's face flushes red. How can a whole day just disappear?

Maggie closes the door behind her. Bewildered, Katie puts her head in her hands and tries to sort through the fog.

~

"HEY, GIRL. HOW'D IT GO?" Sam calls from the kitchen as she hears Katie put her bag down in the front hall.

Katie hangs her coat on a hook and walks into the sun-yellow kitchen.

"I don't know." *Honesty is best,* she thinks.

"Well, that sounds positive." Sam scrunches her face. "Not."

"Um, night shift?" Katie asks, observing the small plastic containers that surround Sam. They are filled with every snack imaginable, from trail mix to cheese cubes. "What's with all the health food? Trying to prove Carly wrong?"

"Yep." Sam snaps the lid shut on a container of almonds. "If I don't have these, I'll end up at the vending machines." She pats her stomach. "And the calories I want to consume don't come until Saturday—bar night!"

Katie smiles. Sam's bar nights are epic.

"You should come with me. Get out." Sam places her snacks in a canvas lunch bag.

"I..." Katie sits down at the dinette table.

"Babchi would approve." Sam looks pointedly at Katie. It's a dare.

Katie breaks eye contact, suddenly feeling cold. "I'm going to go take a hot shower."

"You can't hide forever, Kat."

Katie shuts her eyes tight against the tears and walks away.

8

----

## ANNA

Ghostly, pale light warms Anna as their third day on the truck begins. She slept a little. Two more families were forced to leave their homes and shoved into the back of the truck. Anna wonders what the next stop will be and pulls her sleeping sister close to her. The new prisoners confirmed some of the rumors Anna's father heard back in their town: families were being taken from their homes and shot or exiled from the land they'd lived on for generations. Why? Anna looks down the length of the truck at her father speaking softly to one of the other men. Her father held the lowliest of government positions, and yet they were deported as enemies of the Soviet Union.

The rambling road turns smoother, and Anna hears the sound of trains in the distance. Her heart rises. *Where will we be sent?* They no longer have a country.

Magda wakes groggily, and Anna reaches in her pocket for the last chunk of bread. She puts a finger to her lips and passes the bread to Magda. The girl silently tears off a bite, concealing her meal under a top skirt. Anna's stomach growls jealously.

The truck rolls to a stop at an intersection. Poland, or what used to be Poland, is surrounded between many other countries: Germany, Lithuania, Latvia, the Soviet Union, Romania, and Czechoslovakia. Anna looks ahead to the train depot. If Russia and Germany have annexed Poland, then is any other country safe? The tracks reach out in every direction.

Magda finishes the last meager bite of bread. "It is very flat here," she says, straightening up to look around. The cool morning air has made her hair curl. Anna smiles and smooths it back, combing the blond wisps with her fingers. She separates her sister's hair into sections and begins to weave two braids. They can at least try to keep it clean.

"Isn't this land strange, Anna?" Magda asks, trying not to wince as her sister pulls through a knot.

"Mmhmm. Different from our home. Look at the mountains in the distance."

Magda turns to the east and sees large shapes against the low, cloudy sky. "Do you think we're going there?" Magda squeaks out.

Anna is about to answer, but a young soldier points his gun at the families in the truck and orders them to move out. Anna is beginning to understand the short Russian commands and quickly ties off her sister's braids.

The air is dewy, and mist settles on their clothes as everyone disembarks. Anna wishes she could lick the water off. They haven't had a drink since last night.

"Move." The soldier gestures for the families to walk to a large wooden train depot.

Anna holds Magda's hand while Beata helps her father and mother gather the twins.

"Faster." The harsh Russian makes Anna wince. A soldier dressed in a long olive-green trench coat with red lapels prods Anna in the back with his gun. Biting her tongue, she picks up her pace, attempting to create distance between her and the weapon. The soldier matches her new pace and continues to hold the gun tight against her back.

The train depot is large, with tracks from all directions intersecting in a circle. Anna and Magda try not to stumble over rails as they walk to the building where crates and bins of food and water are stocked. Anna looks away. She knows it is not for them. The guard at her back moves away and joins a group of soldiers smoking cigarettes around a water barrel. Anna's small group is stopped before a long cattle car on the tracks. She does not hear the bellowing of cattle; all she hears are pleas for food and water. The man in front of her moves, and she sees hands stretching out from between the metal bars of the small, rectangular ventilation windows. They look filthy. Anna squeezes Magda's hand.

"*Spragniony.*" "*Chory.*" "*Głodujący.*" "Thirsty." "Sick." "Starving."

Anna turns slightly and sees her father and mother being corralled into the car. Closer, the smell of human waste and sweat is overpowering. Magda is pressed, trembling, against Anna's side. The young girl's eyes widen as she watches urine trickle out from the bottom of the train car and splash on the tracks.

"I can't," Magda says and pulls Anna's arm backward.

Anna swoops down and catches Madga's face between her hands. "We must. Remember what the man told Father on the truck. Families taken by the Germans were shot. We are still alive."

Magda calms and presses closer to Anna again.

"Stop." The soldier places his gun across Anna's chest, barring her and Magda from joining her mother, father, and siblings. She stops as ordered and waits in front of the cattle car with a big "six" painted on the outside.

The soldier takes his gun off Anna when they hear shouting from one car down. Anna and Magda watch as a tall, thin man runs away from the train. He veers left and then right, looking to cross the tracks. Shots fire. Shouts echo from the cattle cars. Then there is brief silence followed by slaps of congratulations. The distracted soldier has his back to the girls, so Anna picks up her sister and hands her to Beata already in the car. Then she hoists herself in.

The soldier turns back to the car, shouts "Full," and draws the door shut.

Anna takes a final breath of fresh air and then turns with Magda to face the crush of bodies. Her eyes adjust to the darkness. "Stay close."

Magda whispers, "I have no choice."

Anna sighs. "That is true, *kochana*."

"We'll move to the back," Anna's father says, reaching over to tap Anna's shoulder. They push through the press of bodies where people sit knee to knee or stand shoulder to shoulder. The air is thick with sweat and body odor. In the far back corner, the press of bodies eases. Most of the people are crowded up front around the small-barred windows.

"Here." Anna's father pats a spot against the wall for the small children to sit. They obey, quiet from shock and awe. Anna pulls Magda onto her lap, her back against the wall. *Safer to see what happens up front,* she tells herself. When she turns her head, the smell of hot feces accosts her. A frail woman is crouched over a small hole cut through the train car floor a few feet away. Everyone around her pretends not to notice. The smell mixes in with what must be days of human waste. Anna's stomach roils. She feels a grip of panic close in around her chest.

"I'm thirsty." Magda looks up at Anna with eyes like large blue pools.

"I think I see Jurek." Anna's father looks at Anna before casting a quick glance at his wife, who sits pale and unmoving. *Like a statue,* Anna thinks.

"Anna and Beata, keep an eye on your siblings." Her father turns and pushes his way through the crowd, more gently this time, stopping to peer into everyone's faces, trying to recognize friends through layers of grime, dirt, and fear.

# KATIE

"Ahh, here's my zombie librarian." Maggie pops her head into Katie's small office.

"Oh, hey." Katie looks up from the rows of information on the spreadsheets before her.

"So, you working on the upgrades?" Maggie walks in and plops herself down on the chair facing Katie's desk.

Katie sighs and waves the pile of sheets in the air.

Maggie arches an eyebrow and sits back. Katie knows the look. A lecture is coming. Or maybe something more. Maggie may look sweet, but she's a Scorpio. She will only let you go so far before she calls you out on your bullcrap. It doesn't matter if you're family, a friend, or a library patron. Sometimes her brute force approach causes more damage than good, and Katie hopes this isn't one of those times.

"If you need help sorting out which computer stations need replacing, let me know. The grant money has to be used up soon. Can't miss the deadline."

"I know that." Katie's head starts to hurt.

"Well, our shiny never-leaves-her-office director wanted to make sure you remembered."

"Since when do you take orders from Dana?" Had new allegiances been forged in the two weeks Katie was out? Even though she's been back for a few months, she hasn't returned to the swing of office politics. She knows she should try. Libraries are a hotbed of high-school-style cliques, complete with backstabbing and banishment.

"The day I start taking orders from Dana is the day I lock myself away," Maggie says and flicks a stray lock of hair from her eyes. "I'm kind of worried about you."

Being straight and to-the-point is Maggie's best quality. Katie appreciates it over the backroom, gossip-girl approach.

"I—" Katie starts to disagree, then cuts herself off. "Yeah, it's hard." The truth spoken in the stillness of her stuffy office brings tears to her eyes. This isn't what Babchi would want for her. *My angel, my darling,* she hears Babchi's voice telling her. *Don't cry. Don't cry.* Tears leak from the corners of Katie's eyes.

"Here." Maggie pushes the box of tissues closer.

"Thanks." Katie reigns in the sadness, pulls a tissue out, and dabs at her eyes. "I mean, it's been three months. Three months!" Katie waves her hand over the piles of work still left to be addressed. "Every morning I wake up and for a split second I think, 'Better hurry, have to stop by and get Babchi's breakfast ready before work.' And then..." She pauses and looks at Maggie with wide, red-rimmed eyes. "Every. Single. Day."

"I know."

And Maggie does. Fifteen years Katie's senior, Maggie has been a widow for seven years, yet the pain of watching her husband suffer and the loss of him remain.

"But," Katie heaves, "when does it stop?"

"There is no limitation on grief," Maggie says. These are the words Katie doesn't want to hear.

Through a wan smile, Katie wipes at her eyes and asks, "Will you walk me through which computers you want to retire? We have enough funding to replace three."

"Guess we'll have to make do."

"Yes," Katie agrees. "We have to make do."

10
___

## ANNA

The train cars, overfilled with misery, leave the station at dawn the next day. Anna feels the heave of the steam engine and opens her eyes, her head resting against her father's shoulder.

"Now it begins." Her father nods at her and gets up to comfort the sobbing twins. Hungry and thirsty, no one has eaten or had a drink for over twenty-four hours. Yet that doesn't stop the pain in Anna's bladder. She has to pee but does not want to expose herself over the hole in the floor crowded in by all these strangers. Magda stares wide-eyed into the mass of dark shadows. Her sister will have to go, too.

"Let's *go*."

"Where?"

Anna points over the sea of bodies, some still sleeping propped up against each other. There is a noticeably empty space around the bathroom hole.

"No, no. I can't. Not in front of everyone."

Anna surveys the car. There is only one hole. People near the hole have their backs to it and collars turned up against the stench. Anna braces herself and takes Magda by the hand.

"We have to." She looks over at her father and mother, who are trying to calm the twins. Beata sleeps up against the wall, having tended to the small children all night.

Magda notes the steel in Anna's eyes and rises, allowing her sister to pull her through the crowd. The smell of the hole grows with every hard-earned step. In the corner, only a few feet away, Anna spots a school friend, Tomasz. He nods his head and politely looks down. Anna's face flushes with embarrassment, which quickly turns to anger. Who is the Soviet Union to exile Anna and her family? Indignation rises in her, and she squeezes Magda's hand. This will not break her.

"Me first?" Magda tugs at Anna's hand, looking both nervous and expectant.

"Yes." Anna leads the girl forward. The hole, big enough to allow a child or gangly teen to fit through, is encrusted with human waste. Even if they could squeeze through, the moving train would crush them. And if the train was stopped, the soldiers would shoot them.

"Here." Anna positions herself in front of her sister to offer some privacy. "Just keep your skirts low. Then no one will see."

Magda blinks back tears. "But they'll know."

Anna cups her sister's face. "Dearest, pretend you are at home. Pretend you're in the little outhouse surrounded by firs." Anna smiles. "These are not people," she gestures to the crowd around them, "they are trees. They make no judgment."

Magda nods and crouches. Anna turns her back and hopes her speech is enough to convince herself, as well.

After Magda finishes, Anna positions the girl in front of

her, using her skirts as Anna had to create a screen. But as Anna rises from the stinking hole, she notices Tomasz turn and shake his head. But why? Pity? Disgust? Her anger rises again. She grabs Magda's hand and is about to confront the young man but stops as he bends over an elderly woman and rubs her back. He sings sweetly close to her ear. Anna recognizes his grandmother.

Her anger evaporates, and she leads Magda away. They are all the same now. Slaves.

**11**

---

**KATIE**

The large meeting room is filled with the twenty part-timers and five full-time staff that make up the library. The town approved a half-day closure for this meeting. *Has to be bad news for them to close completely,* Katie worries.

"Let's sit over here." Maggie chooses two seats in front next to the rest of the full-time staff.

"Show of solidarity?" Katie asks, eyeing Sally, the mercurial head of circulation. Sometimes Katie wonders if all heads of circulation are as angry as Sally. Their anger makes sense, though, what with being forced to interact with the public's demands every day. Even over in her little computer area, Katie is verbally abused at least three times a week. Comments like "Move faster, I pay your salary" are common.

Sally smiles and glances their way. Typical. One minute she'll scold you for not filing a service request properly, and the next day she's your best buddy because you got the circulation computers back online. Katie gives a small wave and a nod.

The town council and library board president are sitting at the head of the room alongside the mayor and the library director, Dana.

"Hmmm... Dana is not sitting with us," Maggie says, straightening up in her chair.

"Let's get this started," the mayor says, moving to the podium. "Thank you all for coming..."

**12**

---

# ANNA

**Siberia**

After three grueling days of sickness, stench, and only a cup of water and small chunk of bread each day at six A.M., Anna feels the train shudder to a stop. Sunlight and chilly air pour in through the barred windows. The cold air smells clean, and Anna sighs, hoping they will finally be allowed off. She peers through the dim shafts of light in the hazy boxcar and picks out the bodies sprawled on the floor that are no longer moving. She tries to shield Magda's view, but the young girl is thankfully oblivious—excited by their stop and hopeful they will gain some freedom.

Anna wonders what *next* will be. Her father looks tired, her mother remains silent, and the twins are hungry and weeping most of the time. Beata catches Anna's eye and nods to their mother. Beata will care for her. Anna just needs to keep Magda safe. And the twins? They are so small and thin; Anna can't help but think they will not survive long.

The cattle car door creaks open, and Magda starts toward the sunlight pouring in. Anna grabs her hand and pulls her close. "We will stay together." It is an order. "Better to wait and let others go first."

Magda nods and looks back at her father and mother struggling to stand. She clasps Anna's hand tighter.

The soldiers file the prisoners down a well-worn, wooden ramp. The train depot—a large, raised platform in the middle of flat fields—is bustling. Thick forest borders the edges of the fields and continues for miles. The prisoners are herded in front of long, low warehouses next to the tracks. More Russian soldiers push the group together to form a line while an officer seated at a table gestures for the next family to approach. Group by group, their names are checked off the officer's list. Some families are pushed back onto the train while others are led to open, flat-bed trucks. Several dirt roads lead away from the depot to distant hills and even farther mountains.

"*Nazvaniye.*" The officer issues a command.

"Jankowski," Anna's father's rough voice answers with their surname. He glances longingly as three soldiers drink from a barrel of water to the side.

"Enemy of the people," the officer condemns. "Ten years labor."

"My children..." Anna's mother gasps, her family's fate sinking in.

A soldier shoves the butt of his gun into her back. "*Tishina.*"

Anna's father pulls the boys close to either side while Beata puts an arm around her mother and whispers comfort.

The officer gestures them aside, and two guards lead them to a partially filled truck. They hoist themselves up.

One more family joins them, and Anna recognizes their father as another civil servant who held a low government position similar to her father's.

"Bogdan, what will happen to us? Our children?" Anna's mother asks, clutching her husband's arm.

"All Polish nationals. And Poland is no more," the father from the new family says as Russian soldiers jump into their sentry positions and the truck bumps across the flat plains.

13

________

## KATIE

Katie sits in silence, flanked between her siblings and parents. The lawyer drones on, but everyone listens patiently through the will's preamble. Squirming in the hard-backed seat, Katie wonders what Babchi did with her estate. She'd had enough savings to get by, and she owned her house outright. Katie's mind wanders to the library meeting last week. It went down just as she and Maggie feared: their cozy, municipal library was joining the statewide consortium. While this meant better tech support through a centralized system, many jobs were going to be lost. Including Katie's.

The lawyer clears his throat. "Now I'll read through the bequests."

Katie's cheeks flame red. She hasn't told her parents she's been laid off. She can't bear the recriminations. Coming from such an aggressively success-driven family, Katie often wonders if she was adopted.

"Now as you all know, Anna was thrifty. On her husband's meager factory salary, she bought and sold two houses in her lifetime," the lawyer says, finishing up the introduction to the will.

Everyone in the room chuckles. Between Babchi's eye for a good deal and her husband's carpentry skills, Babchi said they could have been rich flipping houses on one of the many house remodeling shows she loved. Katie smiles. Babchi was proud that she was able to create a legacy. It wasn't large by most standards, but to an immigrant who lost even the land she had called home, it was everything.

Katie takes deep breaths in an attempt to unravel the growing knot in her stomach. The shame of receiving anything from Babchi's death makes Katie nauseous. She looks at her perfectly coiffed brother and sister. Each of them have well-stocked investment portfolios. But, as her parents always remind Katie, it was her choice to go into public service. She rubs her temples and wishes she could turn back time.

"To each of my grandchildren, I leave the amount of twenty thousand dollars."

*Wow, Babchi didn't boast for nothing,* Katie thinks. Her small fortune was impossible to detect from the frugal life she lived.

Katie's brother raises an eyebrow and snorts, "Well, that'll take care of property taxes."

"Please, that doesn't even cover a year," Katie's sister says with a frown. "Montclair completed a reassessment, and with the renovation I gave the house this year, I'm looking at a serious increase."

"Not my fault you choose to live in such a high-tax state," Katie's brother pokes.

"Your mansion in the swamps will sink one day," Katie's sister shoots back.

Katie nods in agreement. Building a mansion on old

swampland in Florida was not one of her brother's more prudent choices. But who is she to judge?

The lawyer continues, "I leave my house to my grandchild, Katie."

"Huh, well, talk about a sinkhole," Katie's brother says, snickering like a child.

Katie's face falls. The house? Over a decade ago, after Katie's grandfather died, Babchi moved to be closer to Katie's parents. The house is filled with many wonderful memories, but the necessary renovations are more than Katie thinks she can handle. The house hasn't had any repairs except the new roof Katie's mom insisted Babchi install a year ago. She told Babchi bluntly that she did not want to be stuck selling a water-damaged house. *Well, Mom,* Katie thinks, *now it's my problem.*

Katie's mother turns and gives a smile and a nod. *Great.* Katie's stomach sinks lower. When Mom is happy about something, it isn't usually in Katie's best interest. *Probably wants me closer to her so she can talk me into a more lucrative career. Maybe the nursing talk again, or even worse, the it's-not-too-late-to-become-a-doctor talk.*

The lawyer pauses. "And to my daughters, Karolina and Hanna, for all the help they gave me these last years, I leave the remainder of my estate, including all my medals." Katie isn't too interested in history herself, but she knows her brother must be fuming. He is a collector, and Babchi was awarded a few medals for serving in WWII.

Katie's uncle, sitting off in the corner, lets out an audible sigh.

"Is there something you'd like to say, John?" Katie's mother asks.

"No. Until the very end, our mother remains an enigma." John rubs his forehead.

"How would you know?" his sister, Hanna, says. "Leaving us to take care of her while you were doing—what? Pursuing your hobby? Art?"

"I can help you," Katie's mother says, attempting to derail the argument as much to save face in front of the lawyer.

"I'm sure you can." John stands up. "For a price." He walks over and smiles down at Katie. "I, for one, am not willing to pay it." He kisses Katie on the top of her head and waves a goodbye to her siblings.

"I don't understand," Katie's mother says, shaking her head. "Mother treated us equally." She clutches her husband's arm in a rare display. "I can't help John for the poor choices he has made. I mean, really, who would go into the arts and expect a decent living?"

"I know, dear," Katie's father says, squeezing his wife's hand as Hanna sits stone-faced.

Katie stares after her favorite uncle. He got nothing. What was Babchi thinking?

Everyone stands up to thank the lawyer. Papers are signed. And all Katie can think as she scribbles her name on the dotted line is *What am I going to do alone with that dilapidated old house?*

**14**

---

## ANNA

The soldiers lead Anna and her family to a wooden shack on a hillside. It sits next to rows of similar shacks with dirt paths connecting to a main street in the middle of the shanty town. Barracks line the far edge of the settlement. More fertile land lies to the south in a slight valley surrounded by a thick fir forest.

"You will be picked up at six every morning to work," the lead soldier says, pushing the door open.

Anna watches as her mother takes in the rough-hewn walls, the gritty floor, and the makeshift wall separating a living area from a sleeping area. Wind whistles through gaps in the planks.

The soldiers walk away, their feet hard against the partially frozen ground.

"Bring the twins in," Anna's mother says to Beata before she sits down in an old wooden chair. Her eyes close, and she nods off. Anna's father hands the twins to Beata.

"I'm going to see if anyone from our town and the nearby farms are here." Their father pulls his coat tight and steps out.

"I'll get the twins down for a nap," Beata says to Anna and Magda.

"I can sweep out the hearth," Magda offers, surveying the pile of dust against the blackened hearth. "Do you think there's any wood?" Her eyebrows knot together.

"Don't worry, I'll find something." Anna is determined to get the lay of the land. She knows her father will come back with news of the war and politics, but what Anna needs, what her siblings need, are a fire and something to eat.

"Anna," Beata calls from the bedroom area. Anna walks in, leaving Magda to use a ripped petticoat as a rag to clean the hearth.

The sleeping area is well swept with bundles of straw lining the edges as beds.

"It looks as if a family just left," Beata says. "We'll have to clean those first." She points to a pile of old linen sheets in the corner.

"There's a broom outside the door. But no water," Anna says.

"Yes." Beata walks the twins over to a pile of straw. "Just for tonight, boys. We'll wash up tomorrow."

Anna heads back into the dimly lit room where Magda is rubbing ash out of the hearth. "It isn't too bad," she says, smiling wide, her blue eyes searching Anna's face for comfort.

How can her sister still hold hope? Will she be able to do the same?

Anna smooths back Magda's hair. "It isn't. I'm going to find some water." She kisses her sister on a soot-streaked cheek. "Then I'll look for wood for the fire. Can you check if there's anything usable in the cupboard over there? And then sweep out the rest of the room?"

"Of course," Magda says and gives her sister a quick hug. "Do you think a new family has moved into our house?"

Anna squeezes her sister back and whispers, "We will make it through this."

"I know," Magda says with a nod.

Outside, the brisk air pushes Anna's sadness away. She needs to understand this place. Sentries stand at the main exits to and from the makeshift town. There are no guard towers, but the watch guards' guns block the way to the forest. Anna knows she could survive in the forest. But could she evade the soldiers long enough? *Long enough for what,* she wonders. For the war to end? Does anyone in Europe know what has happened to them? To Poland? *Water first,* she reminds herself. Father will talk to other prisoners and find out whether or not she, or any of them, has reason to hope for their freedom.

# 15

## KATIE

*How am I supposed to fix this place up?* Katie looks around the small kitchen. Industrial, cafeteria-style flooring peels up in the corners. Near the fridge the tiles have disintegrated, showing worn plywood beneath. Katie smiles at the bare patch. She remembers when Babchi left a bag of potatoes out to rot and the caustic mush dissolved the supposedly indestructible linoleum.

The floor creaks softly as Katie walks past the 1940s stove —broken for the last ten years. Babchi used to light a match and hold it up to the burner to ignite the gas flame. The built-in oven was a 1950s homemaker's dream with two ovens and a warmer, plus five burners. But Katie knows it is an archaic nightmare that leaks gas. The estimates and proposals they got to tear out the wall unit or do a complete kitchen renovation were expensive. In the end, Babchi decided the most prudent course of action was to disconnect the leaking ovens and only use the burners. She would make do.

Through the doorway next to the old counter and sink, Katie surveys the sunroom. Freezing in winter and broiling in summer, it is the opposite of energy efficient. She turns away from the problematic room and decidedly ignores a patch of mold growing in the farthest corner.

The front room is better—filled with junk, but structurally sound. Babchi's favorite chair sits empty, surrounded by Polish newspapers and books. The giant old television set across from it hasn't had this much rest since it was purchased. Katie remembers that her grandmother bought the giant tube TV on sale after her grandpa died, just as flat screens were becoming popular. Babchi watched the television non-stop with shows ranging from comedies like *The Golden Girls* to serious documentaries and, of course, her home remodeling shows.

Katie tries to lift the TV. It won't budge. *If only it were a flat screen*, she thinks.

Katie turns and walks to the bedrooms, ignoring the bathroom's moldy ceiling and missing shower tiles. Her grandfather's old bedroom is untouched but filled to capacity with overflowing boxes of clothes, sheets, and rugs. Babchi bought the cheap goods through catalogs and then mailed them to relatives in Poland. Her family never regained their land after the Communists took control, but they managed to keep a small farm in the country. Babchi's parcels filled with Katie's and her siblings' hand-me-downs sometimes clothed a whole village. Katie peers into Babchi's bedroom where the smell of violet perfume lingers. Ada obviously had not cleaned up much of the clutter. Katie takes in the piles of clothes on every surface, and rows of empty cologne bottles, and tears well up in her eyes. Babchi kept the decorative-shaped bottles: a bunny, a bird, a kitten.

*Kitten, why are you so sad?* Babchi's voice echoes in Katie's head.

"Why, why did you leave me with this?" Katie asks, clenching down sadness and pain. "You left me."

*Kitten, come here,* the voice beckons. Katie imagines her head resting against Babchi's shoulder and feels the warmth of Babchi stroking her hair. She calms down. It didn't matter how big or small the problem, or whether it was fixable or not, being with Babchi lessened the anxiety.

No, no more memories. Katie commands the vision to disappear, then wipes her eyes and shuts the door.

**16**

---

**ANNA**

It's dark outside when Anna hears the warning bell. She drags herself out of bed and wakes her sisters. They are lucky that the officer in charge of work assignments changes every day. Each morning confusion reigns, which means Anna has been able to keep her mother from the fields thus far.

Anna looks at her mother lying in bed with her eyes wide open in the dawn light. She has barely slept or eaten for weeks. Anna hopes the morning chaos at roll call continues so her mother will not be missed.

"Get up, Magda." Anna shakes her sister's shoulder. The child could sleep through anything.

Magda brushes the sleep from her eyes. "I'm tired." She states it as a fact, not as a complaint.

Anna sighs and shoves a piece of hard bread into her hand. "Eat this." Beata rushes in to help the girl. They cannot be late.

"Good morning, Ania," her father says as Anna walks into the large room by the hearth. "Coffee?"

"You mean hot water and chicory?"

"Yes, but it warms one up." Her father hands her an old, chipped cup. Sundays were the prisoners day off and Anna did her trading then. She swapped one of her mother's broaches at the black market in the local village on the other side of the hill. The market was always bustling on Sundays to take advantage of the labor camp residents. The villagers trade equally with prisoners, soldiers, and guards alike. Anna was able to barter the broach for enough crockery so her entire family could eat together. *If only we had food to fill our plates,* she thinks while sipping the steaming liquid. Anna reminds her growling stomach that she needs to save the remaining jewelry for more important exchanges. The pieces can't be thrown away for sausages and ham, even if that sounds like a good choice in the moment.

Anna glances at the twins huddled next to the hearth. Their noses are running again although the spring weather is sunny with only a slight chill. She picks up each boy, places them side by side at the table, and uses a wet linen to wipe their faces clean.

"Mother?" Beata has Magda dressed and ready at the door. "Mother?" Beata asks again, hoping to break through her fog. "The twins can have one portion of the potatoes for lunch." Beata wasn't searched yesterday after working in the fields. She smuggled four old potatoes in her skirts. After planting the tiny eye sprouts in their garden, she boiled the remaining tubers into an edible mush.

"Come, Beata," their father says as the final bell rings through the camp. "Your mother will manage."

Anna locks arms with Magda and leads her out into the cold dawn. A red sun peers over the horizon as families—children, mothers, fathers, and grandparents—stumble into their work groups.

There are a few hundred prisoners in the labor camp. Their crime? Living on land that the Soviet Union coveted. Quickly, the groups are put into wagons, given their food ration, and driven to the fields. Everyone bites carefully into the hard, small roll of bread. Many of the prisoners have broken teeth on the bread, and Anna noticed that people disappeared after infection set in. She reminds Magda to slow down and soften the bread in her mouth first.

ANNA and her sisters will work in the potato fields again. Their father is assigned to a men's group cutting wood in the forest.

As Anna digs in the fields, she ignores the pain rising from her red, cracked hands and nails caked hard with mud. The ground is softening from the last spring frost, but even in June the earth holds some of winter's cold.

In the next row over, Magda, small and quick, pounds at the soil with a ceramic shard she found at the field's edge. The soldiers provide no tools. Prisoners have to make their own or dig with their hands. Anna is grateful Magda is too young to notice the way in which some of the women prisoners gain favors in order to obtain tools or be dismissed from work. Anna keeps careful track of which woman is keeping which soldier or officer company. She doesn't want to cross paths with anyone's favorite.

*If only I could find lotion or grease on the black market....* Anna's mind wanders as a way to distract herself from the pain, but her escape is short-lived. Soon, images of the past months crowd her mind: the twins lying in bed burning with fever, her father forced to work while sick, all of them left with a lingering cough, and the twins pale and drawn. Anger rises in Anna's throat as her tears dissolve on her flaming cheeks. While digging, she glances at the guards hovering around the field. They are well-fed and warm, wrapped in spring coats. But she and a hundred other women and girls dig in the soil on their hands and knees. Slaves. Her hands grab fists of earth as she looks at Magda, a schoolgirl, dirt-streaked with a shawl wrapped around her head to keep the chill out.

The butt of a rifle pushes into Anna's shoulder. She does not make eye contact but keeps her head down and works faster to drop a potato eyelet into a hole before moving to dig another. The guard, unsatisfied, pulls her face up in his rough hands and peers into her eyes. She stares blankly, taking in short breaths, trying to show neither fear nor defiance. The guard nods and drops her head. Anna trembles as the guard walks back to his post. She is glad that she did not wash this morning. Her face, red and smeared with grime, must be unappealing. Smiling, she ties the shawl closer under her chin and works faster down the row past the older women. She knows what happens to the beautiful girls in this unlawful place and silently vows to keep her face unwashed. She will do everything in her power to make sure Magda does as well. How long can she protect her sister as she grows into a woman and becomes more beautiful?

AFTER THE DAY'S WORK, the women are marched back to the shanty town, and Magda meets up with a group of girls her own age. They talk excitedly to each other as if they are walking back from a regular day at school. The guards, tired too, leave the girls alone. Everyone is thinking of tomorrow, Sunday, when normal duties are suspended.

The women and girls pass through the barbed-wire fence and stand for roll call. Finally, they are dismissed to gather any rations they have earned and return home. *Home.* Anna scoffs at the idea.

Magda leaves her friends to rejoin her sisters, and as the girls approach their shack, the sound of the twins' coughing carries through the flimsy wooden door. Inside, a small fire burns. The rough ground is covered with a thick wool rug that Anna bought with another piece of jewelry.

"Mother, it's warm tonight. Agata and Martyna are going to walk into the village," Magda says to their mother who sits soundlessly by the fire.

Beata looks at their troubled mother's face and says to Magda, "Check the camp clock and be back in two hours. And be respectful to the villagers and the guards."

Magda smiles.

"No foolish trades," Anna says, her lips pursing. Last week, Magda traded a day's ration for a hair ribbon. "I'm hungry, too, and can't always share if you are giving your food away."

Magda blushes and nods her head as she ties off her golden braid with a bright pink ribbon.

17

———

**KATIE**

"Long weekend!" Carly bustles into the apartment carrying bags filled with potato chips, popcorn, chocolate bars, and more.

"New diet?" Sam picks out a tub of mint chocolate chip ice cream. "I approve."

"Is it guilty pleasure weekend already?" Katie asks and looks up from her laptop. The lists of job openings are beginning to blur together.

"Yes!" Carly pulls the ice cream away from Sam and places it in the freezer. She waggles her finger and says, "Better than bars every weekend."

"To each their own." Sam rips open a container of chips. "I know these are reconstituted and all, but they are so delicious."

"Mmmhmm." Katie gets up and grabs a stack of chips, shoving them into her mouth. "Yep," she says, crumbs falling, "it's the salt."

"Hey, this is supposed to get me through the three-day weekend." Carly takes the potato chips back. "Unless either of you wants to camp out with me on the sofa?"

Sam and Katie roll their eyes.

"Don't need to see anymore PDA between you and Mr. Wonderful," Sam says playfully.

"We aren't that bad."

"Yes, you are," Sam and Katie say in unison then burst out laughing.

Carly chomps down on some chips. "Yeah, maybe we are."

"Well, tonight is free shots at Harvey's. Want to come?" Sam asks Katie.

"I don't know. I should keep going through the job ads." It has been four weeks. Libraries all over the state are cutting back full-timers, and Katie doesn't think there's a single library job she hasn't applied for.

"Why don't you just work as a school librarian?" Carly asks, offering some more chips to her roommates.

Katie sighs. Carly asks her to work at a school at least every other week. But having watched how even good-natured Carly gets pulled into the school's political drama, not to mention all the parents' demands, Katie knows she wouldn't last a day.

"Tempting, but still no."

"She doesn't want to work for a bunch of bitchy women who ironically almost always work for male principals." Sam is getting her feminist on.

"Okay, okay. I know the data supports you." Carly puts her hands up in mock surrender. "But it isn't all bad. The kids can be really great. And some of the parents..." She winks at Katie.

"You win. One movie." Katie caves.

"I wasn't even really trying." Carly claps her hands. "What should we start with? A trilogy? I have *The Hunger Games.* Or a little history and romance with *Titanic*?"

"If Jack hadn't been so obsessed with saving Rose, he would've made it." Sam rips open a chocolate bar.

"Here we go again." Katie shuts down her laptop.

Carly puts her hands on her hips. "Yes, but then he would've never experienced love...not unlike some people I know."

"Whoa, don't make it personal," Sam says, laughing. "You know I love."

"At least a couple times a month, right?" Katie quips.

"That's not love," Carly moans.

Sam smiles. "But seriously, aside from my own relationship goals."

"Ahhh, *lack* of goals," Carly says, putting the remaining chips and chocolates into the cupboard.

"Whatever. Rose was the cause of Jack's demise. Without her, he would've lashed together a deck chair and an armoire, and bang, he would've had a boat."

"She makes a convincing argument," Katie says, turning back to the two.

"Not really," Carly says and offers a bag of chocolate chip cookies to her friends. "The other people in the water would've grabbed onto the makeshift boat and sunk him."

"Oh, not my Jack." Sam breaks a cookie in two. "He would've been away from the final sinking long before the boat went under. He would've had a head start if it hadn't been for all that nonsense with Rose and the necklace, blah, blah, blah."

"So, *Titanic* it is!" Carly marches into the living room and flips on the TV.

"Thanks a lot, Sam." Katie picks up the cookies and plunks down onto the sofa.

"Guess you wanted *Hunger Games*? I could give my analysis on that one too, you know."

"No, please don't." Katie hands Sam a cookie in exchange.

Carly continues to ignore her friends and starts the movie. The eerie Celine Dion song fills the room through the massive speakers Carly's fiancé insisted on installing.

"See you two later." Sam picks up her phone and heads for the door.

"Make good choices," Carly calls out.

"Always do, always do," Sam answers.

As the door shuts, Katie nestles back into the soft chenille sofa fabric and gets pulled into the murky depths of the past.

# 18

# ANNA

Sobs and screams echo through the shack, leaking into the chilled morning air. Anna wakes with a start and runs to her mother. Beata is holding her close, trying to stifle her screams. It would do no good to wake the guards.

"Mama, *cichy, cichy*," Beata says and gestures Anna to the twin's bed. In the corner pile of straw and covered by a rough woolen blanket, the two boys are still.

"Hush, Mama. Hush," Beata soothes her. Their father is away as part of an overnight detail to clear a portion of the Siberian forest.

"Take her to the fire," Anna instructs her older sister. "Give her the tea." The tea is a concoction of wild herbs Anna collected from the forest on a Sunday while most of the guards were down in the village. A mild sedative, it would calm their mother so that the sisters could leave her safely for their day's work.

Anna hears their mother's sobs subside as Beata forces the liquid down. Magda is sleeping deeply on the other side of the room. They have been weeding the tobacco fields all week. It is back-breaking work that stains the fingers. Anna takes a steadying breath and moves to the twins' bed. The day will start soon, and she doesn't want Magda to see more death.

Looking down at the boys' triangle-shaped, blue-lipped faces, Anna wonders if she could have done any more against the pneumonia that settled into their chests. But there was no cure Anna or the forest could offer them. All they can give is a burial.

Anna grabs two worn sheets and wraps the boys' small bodies. The woolen blanket will now go to their father. He is cold all the time. The jewelry is almost gone, and soon they'll have nothing to barter with.

Anna turns as Magda stirs. The tea has worked its magic, and their mother dozes on a chair next to Beata. Anna lifts the first boy and carries him, then the other, outside.

The shanty town is starting to wake up. A neighbor walks over to help Anna lace up the thin shrouds. The man, a father of three, nods at Anna and picks up one of the bodies. The guards will not be at the west gate before roll call, which means Anna will only have to bribe the guards near the forest edge. She touches the cigar in the pocket of her apron. It would make an excellent trade in the village, but she knows she must use it for this. She walks to the back of the hut and fetches the broken-down wheelbarrow her father mysteriously acquired. The neighbor places both boys' bodies in the wheelbarrow and wishes her well. It would be harder to bribe the guards with him along. Anna thanks him and pushes her brothers over the bumpy back road away from the shacks toward the fir forest. She has to be quick. If the day guards start their morning patrols, she will be caught and her brothers put in the mass grave. But if she hurries, she can use one of the graves the labor camp prisoners already dug in the forest. There is usually one or two. She pushes the wheelbarrow faster.

19

___________

## KATIE

"Is this really what you want?" Katie is angry, her voice louder than she can control. Her mother at the sideboard continues to happily sort pills while Babchi sits in her embroidered wing chair, leveling Katie with her gaze.

"You know what this means." Katie can feel herself spiraling into a terrifying new place. "You know what the medication does." Katie stares into Babchi's eyes. She wants to hear Babchi—her protector, her friend, everything she has ever known a mother to be—say the words: *I am ready to die.* But Babchi gazes back at Katie, her blue-gray eyes sad and full. Grasping the arms of the chair, she nods, her eyes never once leaving Katie's face.

Hot tears form at the edges of Katie's eyes. "I won't stand here and watch." She turns and walks out the door.

Two days later, by the time Katie comes back, Babchi is so riddled with pain and medication, she can't even open her eyes.

"She was the best mother..." Katie snaps back to the present at the sound of her mother's voice. She looks around the cramped room at Far Oaks, the memorial garden near her parents' house. She dashes the tears off her cheeks, relieved she is sitting in the back of the room away from the precious few who have been invited. Controlling Babchi even after death, her mother declared it was Babchi's dying wish to only have a select few share in the family's grief.

"I remember when Anna..." Katie's father is speaking from the podium now. Probably a speech her mother wrote for him, Katie has no doubt. Katie's brother and sister, along with their spouses and children, listen politely. Katie's sister glances at her phone.

"Why are you holding a private memorial?" Katie had asked. "The whole point is for people to be able to pay their respects and to support the family." *Plus, I actually have some friends who would come to support me,* she wanted to add.

"It was her dying wish," Katie's mother had said while scrubbing the kitchen counter furiously.

Katie had wanted to argue back. Carly and Sam would have attended to support Katie. They both considered Babchi an adopted grandmother.

"Enough, Katie. She was *my* mother." Katie's mom had thrust the soapy sponge close to Katie's face. "Mine."

Now, Katie looks at her siblings sitting in the row up front. Her mother didn't even invite their uncle. Doesn't he have a right to be here? Katie is roused from her musings by the sudden silence in the room. Everyone is looking at her, waiting. She can feel her face blush red.

"Would you like to say something?" Katie's mother asks, gesturing at the podium.

Katie glances down at the program, the professionally printed booklet her mother designed. Babchi's full name is scrawled in gold letters across the front. She notes her mother's name is almost as big a font size as Babchi's. *Well, she is Babchi's daughter,* Katie thinks.

*Oh, yes, Mother,* Katie grimaces, *I have something to say.* She wasn't even asked to read a passage and was only mentioned in the "left behind" paragraph at the end of the printed program. Yes, Babchi left her behind. It hurt more than when her mother left her behind decades ago.

Katies stands, and her mother takes a step back to make space at the podium.

"I have nothing to say," Katie says, her cheeks still blazing. She nods her head to the room of shocked family and leaves.

"I STILL DON'T UNDERSTAND why you're so upset."

Katie stops mid-bite of her chicken salad. "Because it's just another time I'm being set up to fail."

Carly shakes her head and reaches for a fry. Their favorite outdoor cafe is bustling with a Saturday lunch crowd. After the disastrous memorial service, Katie needs some girl talk.

"Well, Greg and I would do practically anything to have a house." Carly swallows her bite. "We're both scraping by on a couple of teachers' salaries and can barely afford a condo."

"My situation is different." Katie feels her telltale blush overcome her cheeks. She knows being left Babchi's house is a wonderful gift. Can she find the words to explain the feeling of resentment she has, even with this knowledge?

"I know your family is..." Carly trails off.

"Narcissistic? Manipulative?" Katie suggests.

"Different. I think they have trouble showing their emotions." Carly nods, happy that she has managed to hold on to her trademark positivity. "The house was a way for

Babchi to show how much she loved and needed you. I'm sure your family wishes you well."

Katie rolls her eyes. Innocent Carly, trying to find the good even in Katie's dysfunctional family. The scene at the lawyer's office with her uncle replays in her head. Carly doesn't get it—she has a great relationship with her mom, but she never got over not having a dad. Her mom raised her single-handedly, so of course Carly's head is filled with romantic notions of a two-parent household. Katie shakes her head at her delusional friend and is struck anew by the fact that the only person who would understand what Katie is going through is gone. Her closest ally and best friend is dead.

**20**

---

**ANNA**

**Summer of 1941**

The Soviet Union switched sides. The news slowly sinks into Anna's brain. Her father sits at their shanty's table discussing the recent events with two fellow Polish workers. Anna's mind races. If the Soviet Union is at war with Germany and has joined forces with the Allies, will they let the Poles go?

"They will not give us our land back." Anna's father's voice intrudes on her thoughts.

She places another branch into the hearth, stoking the small fire while taking in every word. It is Sunday. Her sisters and mother are out for a walk.

"But, Bogdan, the Allies will not allow them to keep us from our land."

The other man scoffs. "You believe the Allies have any power in this? Stalin wants land. He wants to spread his dictatorship across Asia, across Europe. Mark my words, he will not stop with Poland."

Anna's father, looking sallow and drawn, exhales a long puff of smoke from one of their homegrown cigarettes. "Yassick is right. They will not stop with Poland."

"But our army—surely, they will set us free," the other man continues optimistically.

"We no longer have a country. It has been taken from us," Yassick counters. "The Allies will make concessions for the use of Russian forces, but they will not help us."

"Surely, you do not mean you believe us to be Russian slaves forever?"

"Yes." Anna's father looks through the smoke at his daughter. "The real question is: when there is a chance for one to break free, will the opportunity be taken?"

Anna looks away from her father's gaze. She does not like what he is proposing. Would she be able to leave him behind? Or her sisters? How would they survive without her?

Anna's mother shuffles through the front door. The men instantly rise and doff their caps. Her mother neither acknowledges them nor looks away but continues to stare at the ground. After the twins' deaths, she rarely speaks. The only people she will look in the eyes are their father and Beata.

Anna watches, her hands clenching into fists, as Beata guides their mother to a chair. Magda walks in, pulling a heavy bundle of firewood. Yassick, seeing her struggle, hurries to help. Anna notices his fingers linger a little too long on the girl's hand. Magda smiles.

Dread adds to Anna's anger, and she rushes over to carry the wood herself. She must get Magda away from this place. Her little sister needs school. She needs a future. What she does not need is to live and die—or worse, have children—

in a labor camp. Anna places the firewood in the corner and waves a polite goodbye to her father's friends. Leaving Beata to prepare the weak broth for dinner, Anna steps outside. Her father is right. When the opportunity shows itself, she must be ready to leave. And she will take Magda with her.

**21**

---

## KATIE

I t's Saturday. Katie wakes up late to avoid her roommates. On beautiful spring days, Katie remembers the rose garden she and Babchi visited each year to celebrate their May birthdays. She can almost smell the sweetness of the tiffany roses and the spicy undertones of the blood red climbers.

"Babchi, do you have to smell every single one?" Katie asked during a visit. Babchi would walk slowly down each path smelling the rainbow of blossoms. When Katie hurried her, Babchi would simply smile and continue to inspect the flowers.

"Katie, look," she would say and point to a sherbet-colored rose. "When the flower starts to fade, it is a different color."

Katie pictures Babchi during their last visit to the garden. She was dressed in a blue top and blue skirt that had an undulating print like ocean waves. *Quite pleasing for something bought from Babchi's favorite local thrift shop,* Katie thought.

"They are pretty," Katie murmured while yearning to

move at a faster pace. With every passing year, Babchi took longer and longer to observe the flowers, mesmerized by the sheer quantity of roses. No one else in the family would go with them. It was a full day commitment.

"Ahhh," Babchi would say after sniffing a particularly fragrant rose. "It smells different from when it is first open and when it is about to fall."

Katie would press her nose to the flower obligingly, noting the different scents on the same shrub. "I love the climbers." And she did. They bordered the edges of the garden in bursts of red, white, and yellow.

"We will get there. We will get there," Babchi promised Katie as she moved onto the next rose bush, although it seemed to Katie that it was the exact same rose as the previous one she had critiqued.

Sometimes Katie was impatient. She wanted to be moving, seeing things faster. Always faster. But Babchi loved the slow pace of the gardens. She told Katie that as a girl she wanted to be a forester like her father. When Katie asked why she hadn't become one, Babchi simply said, "The war."

After smelling each flower, Babchi would straighten with a small groan. As she aged, her back was a constant source of pain. They hadn't known it was the cancer spreading.

LATER, Katie's roommates interrupt her day.

"We had a great time thrifting," Carly says, taking in Katie sitting with a bag of chips on the sofa. "And you could've used a day out, you know. You're going to start growing mold."

"Why don't you come out tonight?" Sam asks, looking

gorgeous in tight black jeans and a brilliant green shirt. Last year she found a stylist who specialized in curly hair, and it was paying off. Her short curls are expertly gelled, framing her delicate features that have inspired more than one ER patient to comment that she looked like a pixie or an angel, depending on their belief system.

Katie shrugs her shoulders. She hasn't heard from her family since the memorial service. It has been weeks.

"Who knows? Maybe you'll find a lead on a job," Sam suggests.

"Yeah, like bar hopping and dancing is a great place to interview."

Sam laughs. "Information technology people are everywhere! You never know."

"Umm, you do realize that I'm still a librarian, not some corporate hustler or IT guy."

"Open your mind. You could run a corporate office just like I could get out of the ER and be a floor manager or do private care. We're flexible." Sam shakes Katie's shoulders. "Well, we should strive to be flexible." She starts to massage the knots out of Katie's shoulders. "Now go get ready."

"You're hard to argue with," Katie says. It's true she hasn't been out in months. And she only has a couple of months left before she loses her job. At work, prepping all the computers and databases for transfer to the statewide IT team has been particularly depressing. "Alright, let me put something better on."

"Yeah, yoga pants are not the best outfit to get us free drinks. And a shower would really, really help, too." Sam winks and fetches a glass of water from the kitchen. "All about the hydration."

**22**

---

## ANNA

Summer is ending. Anna etches another check mark on the crude calendar gouged into the wall. Soon they will face a second winter in the same dingy hut. It's quiet without the twins. Her mother sits by the small fire staring into the flickering flames. She works in the fields with her girls but mostly keeps to herself. In the very early hours, just as day breaks, she visits the twins' grave. Luckily, she has not been caught by the NKVD, the secret police.

As the war continues, more and more of the NKVD are stationed in the remote area. Many blend in with the village folk, and Anna can no longer distinguish informants from friends. Yassick had been caught. Anna shudders at the memory. He bribed a man who smuggled prisoners over to the next village; from there, it is easier to board a train unnoticed. But both men were shot a few miles down the road. None of the prisoners in the labor camp know who exposed their plan, but people have been much more careful since the murders. Starvation makes men and women participate in unthinkable betrayals. Anna sometimes wonders whether or not, if given the opportunity, she would do the same.

Rumors circulate that, between the NKVD and Russian officers stationed in the village, it isn't safe to trade at the black market anymore. Anti-Polish resentment has risen with Russia's defection to the Allies' side and as the war wears on and food dwindles, many villagers view the Poles as a threat. The Russian officers waste no time in shooting prisoners for real or imagined transgressions, and too many of Anna's friends and her sisters' friends lay piled in the mass grave on the edge of the forest. Many are the last in their family line, with no one left to mourn them.

Not that anyone has energy to mourn. Anna glances at her father, tall and thin, his cheekbones jutting out in hard lines.

"Papa." Anna places a hand on his shoulder.

"Yes, Ania?" He turns and smiles at his daughter.

"Do you want another cup of chicory?"

He pats her hand. "No, no. Make sure you leave some for your mother." He stands, his once-straight back bowed. "I will make my way to roll call." He kisses her on the cheek.

Beata walks Magda into the room and sits her in front of Anna. Anna pulls an old comb through Magda's hair and weaves it into two golden braids.

"What did you say?" Anna asks as Beata says something under her breath.

Beata sighs and points to the roll their father left for their mother at dinner last night.

"Father can't afford not to eat," Magda says, her eyes bleary from lack of sleep.

"No, he can't," Anna agrees.

Beata pours their mother a cup of chicory.

"Thank you, Beata," their mother says, sniffing the

savory drink. "You girls split that roll. I've told your father not to worry."

Beata picks up the roll and splits it into thirds, giving each sister a piece.

"Thank you!" Magda gulps down her bread and stands up with her hair finished.

Anna watches as her dainty mother sips the hot drink. *She could trade her time with an officer for food.* As soon as the rebellious thought arises in Anna's mind, she squashes it. No, her mother married their father for love and would never betray him. *But,* Anna's sneaky thoughts continue, *if their mother was a well-fed, kept woman, she could help her family survive, too.* Anna winces. Would she be able to trade her body if needed?

The bell rings from the main square.

"We better hurry," Anna says. "I'm always amazed by your care," she adds as Beata dumps the morning cups into the wash basin. She cleans the shack like it is a home rather than a temporary prison.

"You care, too," Beata says. "Tonight will be hard, though, with Father away." She gestures to their mother.

Anna nods in agreement. The last time their father's work detail was deployed for a week-long tree harvesting, their mother could not sleep. It fell to Beata and Anna to soothe her through the night.

"I will be fine, my girls," their mother says, rising from her chair and reaching for her shawl.

"I don't mind," Beata says quickly.

"Do not worry so much like your father."

"Come on, Magda, I don't want my rations taken away again," Anna calls, turning from Beata and her mother's argument. She finds Magda in the corner squinting into their small handheld mirror. "What do you think you're doing?"

Magda looks up with pink cheeks and wispy tendrils of hair curled to frame her face.

"You are not going to the fields like that," Anna says, pulling the mirror out of her hands.

With berry juice lightly staining her cheeks and lips, Magda looks much older than her twelve years. Anna sighs. Since her birthday, the girl has become obsessed with her looks. She and her friends steal away any moment they can to catch glimpses of themselves in the river.

"You don't want the soldiers to notice you, *kochana*." Anna licks her finger and smooths the golden wisps down. She hands Magda a piece of old linen.

"I'm not doing it for them," Magda says, wiping her cheeks with the cloth.

Since her birthday, Magda has also started to pout. About almost everything.

"Here." Beata steps in with a linen bonnet. "Let's put this on your head."

"But it's old and stained," Magda protests. "Stop, I just—"

"Listen to your sister."

The girls freeze. They have not heard their mother discipline them since they became prisoners.

"She knows what she's doing," their mother says, walking over to tie the bonnet. "Pretty does not keep you safe, young one." She pats Magda on the head and takes her hand.

The second bell rings.

"Now, we really must go," Anna says, holding the door open. She grabs Beata, and they all rush out.

# 23

# KATIE

The heavy beat of the music makes the crowd dance faster, bodies pushing into each other. Sam laughs and twirls Katie in a circle. Katie feels the room spinning and finally she forgets everything. It's only her and the music pounding into the hard-tiled floor with each step.

"Thirsty?" Sam yells.

Katie opens her eyes and grabs Sam's hand. Arm in arm, they head to the bar.

"You're not a drinker, right?" Sam raises an eyebrow as her longtime friend picks up another beer.

Katie laughs and downs the drink. She's never really been drunk. *A lightweight,* her friends always teased. Now on her fourth beer, she understands how exhilarating it is—as if life can be good again. She gives Sam a thumbs up.

Sam gulps down a shot bought for her by a man across the bar. She waves a thanks, obviously considering him, then turns back to Katie. "Nah. Too young."

"What?" Katie stares at the beautiful twenty-something:

muscled with short-shaved, light brown hair and big amber eyes. "You're crazy."

"Been there, done that." She loops her arm through Katie's. "You just haven't been out with me since when, right after college?"

"Well then, let's make up for lost time."

Katie and Sam push their way into the middle of the dance floor as a fresh rhythm starts. Katie throws back her head and spins, losing herself in the music, finally feeling free.

**24**

———

**ANNA**

**Spring 1942**

Aloud banging against the door draws everyone's attention one Sunday morning. Anna's father looks up from his chair while sipping a cup of steeped fir bark, a variation of coffee for when chicory is not in season. Anna turns from tending the fire as her mother puts down her steaming cup of St. John's Wort. Magda and Beata are still sleeping.

Anna opens the door unafraid, knowing that a soldier would have kicked the door open. She hopes it isn't another hungry neighbor asking for food. After the harsh winter and dwindling supplies, she and her family are starving, too.

"What?" Anna asks the young boy.

"My father said to give this to you."

Anna accepts the crumpled envelope; its edges are streaked in dirt.

*Tadek's handwriting!* Anna's hand begins to shake. It has been two years since they have heard from her brother.

The boy's eyes dart around the shack's main room, his eyes fixing on the pot of gruel simmering on the hearth.

"Anna, let the boy in." Over the past weeks, her father has given away almost every bit of food Anna managed to trade or steal. He is too gentle, too kind.

"Papa?" Anna's voice holds a question. You never know who is an informant for the Russian army, or worse, the NKVD. Anna has herbs and other treasures for trading hidden in the shack. She doesn't like people snooping around.

"Thank you, sir," the boy says, straightening his back, "but my mother is waiting for me." The skittish boy turns to go, then stops. "Thank you for helping my father." He leaves. Anna closes the door and looks at her father.

"Poitr's boy." Her father picks up his pipe and packs down a pinch of home-grown tobacco. Anna dried the leaves in secret behind the hearth; it is a useful bribe.

"He is surviving then." Anna's mother smiles. Piotr's wife was one of Mother's childhood friends. They grew up together going to concerts and lectures in the city.

"His mother keeps the hope of seeing their father alive for the boy," Anna's father says.

"But she must know the truth." Anna sets the letter down in front of her father.

"Yes, as I suspect the boy does." Piotr had been many levels ahead of her father in local government and was not just a mere forester. He was separated from his family and sent to a reeducation camp. Gossip holds that most Poles do not survive long in reeducation. But through his contacts, Anna's father had managed to get a small parcel to the man early on in his confinement, as well as a letter back to his wife and son.

"My dear, our son lives." Anna's father's face breaks into a smile as he holds up the letter to his wife.

"Read it." Tears stream down her cheeks.

"Yes, please read it, Father," Anna says, silently thanking God for answering her prayers. Her brother is alive. Can he help them?

Her father reads:

"Dear Family,

I am currently stationed with the newly formed Polish Army. We call ourselves Ander's Army, for our illustrious commander is no other than Władysław Anders. The Soviet Union is to be praised for permitting us to join in the fight against our enemies. I am sure you have already heard the news that all Polish men holding government positions are to join us. There is talk of amnesty for citizens in the future, as well. I have enclosed papers to authorize your safe passage, Father.

Please give my love to my sisters and brothers. I know you all must be well, and I look forward to seeing you again someday soon.

Love,

Tadek"

Anna drops her arms to her sides, looking around the room frantically.

"He knows the mail will have been searched. He writes well," her father says.

"But, Father, will you..." Anna starts, the magnitude of the message hitting her. Would her father leave them? She can't imagine surviving another winter. And how will they survive without the meager rations their father's work adds to their own? Or worse, how will they survive without his network, his connections? Charming and sincere, her father is a confidant to many families in the shanty town.

Anna's father walks over to her mother and takes her hand. "What is best for the family."

"Always," Anna's mother replies. Tears continue to run down her cheeks.

"Beata or Anna will go." Anna's father looks at his daughter.

"How?" Anna cannot grasp her father's suggestion.

"We only have one chance." He holds up the traveling papers. "Escape is never easy, Anna. With luck, I believe no one will study the papers too closely. Especially if there is talk of amnesty for all deported citizens. The Russians want us gone. There is opportunity in that."

Both parents look at Anna. Is she willing to accept this challenge? Is she willing to accept this gift?

# 25

# KATIE

The man at the bar buys Katie and Sam drinks. Taking in his lean, tan arms and piercing hazel eyes, Katie knows what she wants. Something new, a fling, a chance to devour life and experience decadent pleasure. Sam holds back, letting Katie take the lead and get closer to the guy. With one flick of her head, she downs a shot.

"Want to dance?" he asks.

Katie takes his hand and winks at Sam. The dance floor explodes in a frenzy as loud bass fills the room. There's nothing soft about this club. Colorful lights strobe, and heat rises from the floor. Katie pulses with the music, rocking back and forth with the guy. She becomes aware of how thirsty she is, and an image floods her head. In her mind, she sees Babchi opening a package of towels she ordered from a home shopping show. Katie had tried to talk her out of it. The quality was never as good as advertised. But Babchi ordered them anyway, and as she unpacked each of the lime green towels, she rubbed the plush material against her face, saying, "Ahh, thick and thirsty."

"Babchi," Katie had said. "That sounds obscene."

"What is this word, obscene?" Babchi asked.

Katie shakes her head, pushing the memory away. She pulls the man closer and rocks faster and faster, leaning into the overpowering beat.

26

________

## ANNA

Anna's thoughts swirl. Escape or stay? Leave her family or watch her beloved older sister leave her? That was the choice. Emotions bubble to the surface as Anna walks out of the shack and to the edge of the forest. Her fingers automatically search her apron pockets for a suitable bribe. It's a slow Sunday, and the sentries accept a couple of homemade cigarettes in exchange for letting Anna pass. Rations for everyone, both soldiers and prisoners, decrease every day as the war rages on. The lowly foot soldiers have only slightly more food than the shanty families.

The woods calm Anna's mind, and the scent of pine needles fills her nose. So many compromises and bargains have already been made without her family's consent. If she leaves now, she may never see her parents or sisters again. If she stays, though, she will forever be a prisoner. And what of Magda? Anna has seen the way soldiers look at her. It's predatory, not like the Polish boys whose stares are filled with a respectful longing. No, the soldiers, who get younger and younger with every passing day of the war, look at

Magda like she's fair game, theirs for the picking. It's only a matter of time before—Anna stops her thoughts there.

A soft wind blows through the trees, and the morning birds sing. Anna can almost trick herself into thinking the war is over and she is back in her home, her fir forest. She leans against a tree and pictures their house. In her mind's eye, she sees her mother set bread on the windowsill to cool while her siblings wait for their father to come back from work. Warmth and comfort and feelings of peace fill her. Will she ever know that again?

Anna wipes tears from her eyes and makes a plea, one last bargain with a god she no longer knows if she believes in. If she agrees to leave, she will take Magda with her. Most soldiers and officers won't pay attention to the slight girl if her hair is covered. Anna knows she will trade anything she has to get her sister to freedom and for her sister to have a childhood and a long life.

The forest sounds start to fade as the sun rises higher in the sky, sparkling on the layer of snow. If she doesn't leave soon, the day guards will come on duty, and she will lose a day's rations—or worse.

Anna walks back to the entrance and nods at the guards smoking their cigarettes lazily. She heads to the shanty town with her mind made up. Anna knows Magda will go with her. The girl wants a normal life, and she is young. She will not understand that she may never see Mama or Papa again. Anna makes a promise, speaking the oath aloud to the emptiness around her: "If we get out alive, I will protect her with my dying breath. Magda will survive."

# 27

# KATIE

Bleary-eyed, Katie hits the snooze button on her phone. She drifts back to sleep, savoring the memory of Kyle's skin on hers. It has been so long. The past two years, she devoted all her free time to Babchi's care. No men, no pleasure, just duty. But now... She stretches awake, feeling the softness of her sheets while imagining Kyle next to her. She could stay in bed with this fantasy all day.

But then she stops the dream short. She could never have him here. Roommate Rule #1: *No men sleep over.* Difficult to follow but necessary to keep the peace.

"Katie?" Carly's voice asks.

"Yep, I'm up."

Carly pops her head in. "I hope so." She looks around at the unusually messy bedroom. "You remember you're going to brunch with me and my aunt? Then—"

Katie slaps her hand to her forehead. "Ugh, I forgot. Dress shopping."

Carly's mouth widens in a huge I'm-going-to-get-married smile. "Yes, we have reservations at two, so it's going to be a fast brunch."

"Can I meet you at the shop?"

"The boutique?" Carly corrects. "Sure, but don't forget to eat. You don't look so great."

Katie's head throbs as she props herself up against the headboard.

"Fun night? Didn't hear you come in," Carly says.

"Yeah, late night." Katie pictures Kyle's messy one-bedroom apartment, herself sprawled on the unmade bed. Her cheeks flush with the memory.

"Mmmhmmm." Carly turns to leave. "I'll see you at two."

**28**

---

# ANNA

**Early Summer 1942**

The opportunity to leave comes suddenly once the snow has melted almost completely. The camp is quieter as two military units are dispatched to the frontlines. In a couple of days, replacement troops will arrive. But the worst officer, a man known for shooting Poles upon seeing their traveling papers, has been re-stationed.

This is their window. They all know it is a miracle that the letter from Tadek was delivered to their camp and into her father's hands. Anna credits her father's kindness in helping other prisoners and their families. Polish men who are granted papers are traveling as quickly as possible to meet up with Ander's Army. Some wives and children try to flee, too, but only a handful make it past the sentries. No one knows how long the Soviet government will honor this new agreement, and anti-Polish sentiment continues to rise.

Anna stares at the papers in her hand. Her father and Beata are not back from the fields. Anna remembers the hope in her mother's and father's eyes. Can she leave?

Magda sits by the fire while her mother pulls a wooden comb through her hair, detangling and checking for lice. Fierce resolve fills Anna's belly; she will not leave Magda.

"Mother?" Anna calls softly and holds her mother's gaze.

"Yes. It is time." Joy and sadness cover her mother's face. She ties off Magda's braids.

"May I meet Beata on the road? I want to show her my treasure," Magda says, holding a tiny button etched with a daisy.

"Yes, of course," their mother says, patting the top of Magda's head.

Once the girl leaves, Anna's mother gathers Anna up in her arms and murmurs, "You are my strong girl. More so than I could have imagined. You," she kisses Anna's cheek, "are up to this journey."

Anna sees her mother, clear-eyed and strong, shimmering with hope that at least one of her daughters will find freedom.

The door opens, and Anna's father walks over to embrace them both. "The sentry posts will have a single guard each starting tonight."

"What about Beata?" Anna asks.

Her father pulls away. "We spoke today. She wants to stay with your mother." He looks at his wife and smiles.

"Mother, Father, I cannot—"

"Stop," Anna's mother says, the sparkle in her eyes crowding out the gray to leave only blue. "You will not let this gift go."

"But Beata and you... I may never see you again," Anna says, her resolve weakening.

"Your sisters will always love you no matter where you are. And we," Anna's mother pauses and puts her hand in her husband's, "we will love you forever."

"Sit with me, Ania." Her father ushers Anna to their table while her mother pours chicory coffee. "You must know the rumors I heard today. The journey will be hard."

Anna sits down, nodding.

"Many men in town did not receive the papers they were due. We may thank God we got ours." He leans into Anna, lowering his voice so no one passing by the thin walls can eavesdrop. "Jurek got word from his cousin. The NKVD are on the hunt for Poles traveling to join Ander's Army." He shakes his head and sips his drink. "They have no reason to, other than the hatred in their hearts. You must be careful."

"I will."

The door bangs open, and Beata walks in with Magda. She looks at Anna and falls into her arms, holding her tightly.

"We will be reunited someday. I know it," Beata whispers into Anna's ear.

"I hope so, Beata, I hope so," Anna says, hugging her back.

# 29

## KATIE

"Hey, sleepyhead." Carly smiles and sits down next to Katie on the sofa.

Katie lifts her head off the pillow, waves, and glances at the clock. It's after one P.M., but she wants to sleep. She was out with Kyle until four A.M. The no-bringing-men-home rule really sucked sometimes.

"The cake tasting is at three."

Katie rubs her eyes. Her last week of work starts tomorrow. "Isn't Sam going?"

Carly pauses. Bad sign. "Well, yes, but you were going to go, too."

"I'm really tired, Carly. And I've got a tough week coming up."

"Yeah, I know." Carly's voice begins to rise. "Besides the whole self-pity thing you have going on, what on earth are you doing with this guy?"

Katie snorts. "Please, have you forgotten being single completely?"

"Sex? Is that all you do?"

Katie sits up. "Judge much? It's not as if you don't enjoy

sex. And not everyone has what you and Greg have." Katie swings her legs around. "It's not even what everyone wants."

"Obviously. Sam—and I mean our party-loving Sam—says Kyle is reckless. What are you doing? You know he's not the right guy for you."

"Of course, he isn't." Katie stands up, ready to take a shower. "But no one is."

"Not this way, Katie, it's not you."

Katie sighs. "Look, I'll go to the cake tasting with you."

"I'm not going to force you. That's for sure."

"Carly, you don't have to. I'm just—"

"I know, grieving."

Sam walks in and surveys her friends' faces. "We know, we know, grieving. But could you stop every once and a while and come up for air?"

"I..." Katie begins, but does not want to start a fight with Sam.

"That's all we're asking," Sam says, pushing Katie to the bathroom. "And you really need a shower." She grimaces and shakes her head. "Now I know why you guys hate me partying so much."

"Okay, okay." Katie allows herself to be pushed into the bathroom and closes the door.

# 30

# ANNA

The house is still. The night guards are on duty through the dark early morning. Anna's mother and father are sleeping soundly after their good-byes and tears from last night. Anna adds her secret stash of tobacco to the bag her mother packed last night. Her mother sewed two remaining pieces of jewelry into Anna's skirts. She pushes her hair into a homely bonnet and looks down at her dirt-smeared skirts. She would pass for a peasant. Tadek's traveling papers are tucked safely in her under-skirts. Anna tiptoes over to Magda sleeping on the edge of the bed and shakes her awake.

"You're coming with me," she says and puts a hand over the girl's mouth. "I left a message in the dirt by the hearth to let Mother and Father know."

Magda's eyes widen.

"If you wake them to say goodbye, they will not be able to let you go."

"It's true." Beata's low voice carries from the middle of the bed.

"I didn't want to wake you up," Anna says, turning to her sister. "But I'm glad."

"It's the right thing, Anna." Beata hugs both her sisters. "Magda, you must listen to everything Anna tells you to do. And someday we will see each other again."

"Promise?" Magda asks, her blue eyes searching for her older sister's in the dark.

"Yes, *moja kochana,* yes."

"It will be dangerous but an adventure. And at the end, you will have school, dresses, friends, and ribbons for your hair," Anna promises.

Beata takes Magda's hand and leads her to the front room. By the low embers of the fire, she cuts off Magda's braids while Anna helps dress her to look young. Anna prays they will make it through the trip with her innocence intact.

The sisters huddle together in the darkness.

"It's time," Beata says. "Mother and Father will be fine."

"I know," Anna says, praying for it to be true.

Magda ties her precious pink ribbon around Mother's old, chipped china cup. "She'll remember me every day."

Anna takes her hand, and they walk out the door, only looking back once to blow kisses to Beata.

At the guard post, Anna bribes the soldier on duty. He is too tired to barter for much, and Anna is thankful. She knows she may have to trade more than she's willing if she wants them both to escape.

The dirt road is hard from the morning frost, and the sun is starting to rise. A pale waning moon dots the sky. Soon, the outline of the village comes into view, but the train depot is on the far side with many Russian soldiers and NKVD. Anna is worried about hiding Magda.

She spots a pair of young Russian soldiers huddled by

the outskirts of the village, smoking cigarettes, and trying to stay awake. It's a better way in than the main road. Anna looks the boy soldiers up and down. They seem like a good bet, resembling the farm boys she grew up with before the war broke out. Boys like that wouldn't ask for anything Anna isn't prepared to trade.

Holding her head up, she takes Magda's hand.

"You are ten," she says.

"Yes, I am ten," Magda agrees.

# 31

## KATIE

Katie throws herself down on the bed and listens to her friends chat away in the kitchen. Carly is happily going over bachelorette party plans. Katie knows sleep will not come easily tonight. Her last week of work was hard. There were sad goodbyes but mostly insincere ones. Katie's friends and family thought her job was easy and that everyone who worked at the library was sweet. She will truly miss Maggie, though. But Maggie is starting a new job this week, and Katie has yet to find anything. Not that she is looking that hard, she has to admit.

Katie picks up her phone and skims through her texts to Kyle. Getting together with him is a sure way to tire herself out so she can get some sleep. Her phone pings a *Yes* to her question, and she heads for the shower. She quickly puts on makeup and a simple, light dress. *It won't be on for long,* she thinks.

"Out on a Sunday night?" Sam asks, looking up from the latest show she's been binge watching. "I got popcorn." She shakes the big bowl of buttery goodness.

"Not tonight."

"Yeah, yeah, I get it. You got something better waiting for you." Sam pauses the show. "But you know he's only okay for now. Long term? He's kind of wild, don't you think?" Sam scrunches her face. "Untrustworthy, I mean. That first night he tried to get us both to go home with him."

Leave it to Sam to state the obvious. "Yes, he's my *right now*." Katie feels grumpiness set in. Partying Sam is lecturing her? "He doesn't have to be forever."

"I'm not saying we haven't all escaped reality once in a while, but...I don't know. Just don't get too caught up with this one."

"I won't." Katie feels unsettled and takes a step to leave.

"Carly is really hurt, you know."

"What now?" Katie hangs her head to the side. "Carly is in bride mode. I go to all the events. What else does she want?"

"Whoa," Sam says, holding her hands up in mock surrender. "I'm not getting involved in this one. But she is marrying a great guy. And we're her best friends."

"Yes, everyone knows Carly has a great guy. Picture perfect. Together since grad school." Katie feels heat in her cheeks. "And who are you to give me advice? How many one-night stands have you had?"

Sam stays silent.

"Yeah that's right. And Kyle is not a one-night stand. It might not be traditional, but he's there for me. He's not just a one-off."

"Well," Sam says and shrugs her shoulders. "This is not how I wanted to spend my Sunday night." She turns the show back on. "Have a good night. And just so you know, we —your friends—are here for you, too. Always have been."

Katie leaves. Just like Sam to give a whole bunch of shit

and then shutdown. *She can dish it out but she can't take it,* Katie thinks, slamming her car door shut.

*Damn it.* Katie hates fighting with her friends. A memory interrupts her thoughts: Babchi's warning. The scene plays back in her mind...

"It will change," Babchi said, sitting on the sofa with her arm loosely around Katie's shoulders. It was the year before her cancer diagnosis when they thought she was simply slowing down due to old age.

"I know, I don't expect it to stay the same. But once Carly gets married, we'll never see her."

"You cannot live like girls forever."

"That's not what I mean."

Babchi patted her shoulder and laid Katie's head down in her lap, a leftover gesture from when Katie was a child. Smoothing Katie's hair, she said, "It is natural. Carly wants her own family."

Fear bristled inside Katie. Why hadn't she met someone? She loved children. It was the men that weren't so great.

"You will see. You will find someone, too." Babchi continued to stroke her hair.

"It's not that simple."

"Yes and no," Babchi agreed, pushing Katie up to a sitting position. "Now, let's make a party."

Katie laughed. It was Sam's birthday, and the girls were coming over for cake. Katie picked up a pack of streamers and some tape. "Yes, let's make a party."

# 32

# ANNA

The young Russian soldiers turn to Anna as she walks up to them.

"Excuse me, my sister and I need some assistance." Anna smiles, hoping her intuition is correct.

The two soldiers look at each other, and the taller, curly-haired one asks, "What do you need?"

"Some place discreet to wait until the next train going west pulls in." Anna offers the bare minimum of information. The less others know, the better.

"What do you have?" the smaller blond boy asks.

Anna takes out a few homemade cigarettes.

"Not enough," the taller boy says. He looks Magda over from head to toe. Her face is mostly hidden by the dirty bonnet. He turns back to Anna. "A little more." He beckons the two sisters to follow.

Anna squeezes Magda's hand, willing her to understand they may have to run.

The blond boy walks next to them, chatting easily about the warming weather and how he misses his family. The two soldiers were drafted to Siberia, forcing them to leave their families to struggle on their farms alone.

"This war is messy. First, we are fighting alongside the Führer, and now we are against the Germans." He smiles at Anna. "But in the end, the Soviet Union will prevail. Mark my words."

Anna fights down the angry words forming in her mouth; instead, she smiles demurely as the tall soldier opens the side door to a storage building.

"Here. Wait behind these boxes until we come to fetch you," the tall soldier orders. He leans in close to Anna's face and steals a kiss before walking out of the building with his friend.

Magda shudders. "Yuck."

"Shhh," Anna instructs. "We don't know who else is in here."

Anna pulls aside a few empty burlap sacks from the tops of boxes and covers up herself and her sister.

"Imagine how quickly we could've planted with these," Magda says, pointing to a crate filled with farming tools.

"Hush." Anna wraps her arms around her sister and strokes her hair. It must be sometime around five A.M., and Magda should rest. Anna drops her hand when she hears her sister breathing evenly, asleep.

Her parents will be awake by now and have found Magda gone as well. She prays for forgiveness and hopes Beata can soften the loss. They have lost so much already.

In the darkness, a memory fills her mind. One Christmas their whole family visited relatives in Warsaw. The massive cathedral was awe-inspiring, but the priests...Anna shakes her head at the thought. She couldn't believe the splendor they lived in. The men were plump and dressed in fine, embroidered robes. She was envious—envious that men had created a world where they had choices with rights that entitled them to food, shelter, and clothing, just as the officers at the labor camp have done. Anna longs to be someone else, to have freedom to choose her path. She longs to be anyone but herself in the here and now.

A train whistles far off in the early sunrise, and Anna hears footsteps outside that break her reverie. The two young soldiers are at the door with a friend. Anna hides the view of Magda's face from them and walks over.

The three soldiers cram into the small building, looking both shy and hungry at the same time. Anna is afraid the time to barter has arrived.

"Lift your blouse," the tall soldier commands.

In broken Russian, Anna negotiates: they can see her breasts, but that is all. Then they will help the sisters onto the incoming train. The tall soldier, the oldest one of the three, Anna guesses, wants more. They argue back and forth. Anna is aware precious time is passing, so she ups the ante and strikes a deal. Keeping eye contact, Anna watches as two soldiers fondle her breasts while the third stands lookout by the door. She raises her hand slightly to cover herself as one bends his face in. She breathes out in relief when he backs off.

Satisfied, they point to the door and tell Anna the freight train will stop at the station in ten minutes. It's up to Anna and Magda to run onto the train when they see a chance. The blond-haired soldier will scout for NKVD so the girls can leave their hiding place safely. Anna is relieved they do not push her more and fixes her blouse.

"Magda, wake up," Anna says, shaking her sister. "The freight train will be here soon." It's a safer choice than a passenger train.

"Mother, Father," Magda says with sleep in her eyes.

"Shush. They will be overjoyed when they receive a letter from you telling them all about school and how you are getting the best grades."

Magda nods her head.

"I will keep you safe. Always."

The train whistle sounds in front of the station, and its brakes squeal to a stop.

"We can do this." Anna stands, ready for the soldier's signal to leave the building. "Ready?"

Magda grasps her sister's hand. "Ready."

The door opens, and early morning light rushes in.

# 33

## KATIE

Katie still feels the pulse of the club music in her body. *Maybe one too many shots,* she thinks groggily, *but I'll sleep it off.* Kyle lays her on the bed and kisses her neck, working his way down and discarding her clothes as he goes. She tugs off his shirt. Even after all these weeks with him, she remains in awe of his muscled chest. Katie's past boyfriends were a string of sci-fi-watching nerds. She really liked them, but none had ever been inside a gym.

Being in bed with Kyle with his naked skin against hers, she feels nothing but the moment. *Here and now,* she thinks. *That'll be my new mantra.* Lost in sensation, she matches his rhythm, and in the back of her head she registers a slight tug on her neck. Is her necklace caught? She feels more pressure. She ignores it; she can buy a new chain if it breaks. Her breath becomes shallow, and her mind begins to cloud. She only feels bursts of touch and tingling sensations. There's a constant tightness on her neck, but she doesn't care; she is light and pure pleasure. She cannot form any words as her body explodes into release. Floating back down to earth, she takes in big gulps of air. Her head is pounding, and there's a painful flashing light behind her eyes. Kyle is gazing down at her, his eyes triumphant. His eyes are...predatory?

"That was beautiful."

Katie pushes Kyle to the side and sits up. Rubbing her temples, she touches the chain with Babchi's ring on it still intact around her neck. Did it get caught? Was it an accident?

She looks at him. No, he wouldn't have done that on purpose. Katie's thoughts jumble, and Babchi's words of warning echo in her head: *You are too feeling. You trust too easily.*

"I have to go." Katie is startled by her hoarseness.

"So soon?" Kyle grabs Katie's hand. "There's so much more we could do."

"I can't." Katie pulls on her clothes quickly. "I have to find a job. I have to—"

"Whoa. It's four A.M. Not many librarian jobs going at this hour."

*Why am I here?* Katie looks around in a panic, grabs her purse, and walks to the door. She pauses. "Don't call me."

"If that's what you want," Kyle says, still sitting in bed.

"Yeah, I think—no, that's what I want." Katie leaves the apartment and doesn't look back.

# 34

# ANNA

The freight train rattles and huffs through the early morning hours. Magda sits silently, gazing out the barred window. The last train ride that took them to Siberia is imprinted deep in both of their minds.

Anna leans back and closes her eyes for a moment's rest while they speed away, far from the cold and the starvation. The young soldiers were as good to her as she could have hoped. Before the sisters jumped on the train, the blond soldier had even told Anna that Ander's Army was rumored to be organizing in Uzbekistan. She prays the information is current and looks down at her tired body. Funny, she thinks, how she used to curse her thick build, her strong muscular thighs, and short lean arms. *Lucky for me, this strong peasant body will keep me alive.*

"What's so funny?" Magda asks, her reverie broken by her sister's laughter.

"Just thinking how strong we are," she says, not realizing she had laughed out loud.

Magda, with their mother's honey-gold hair and deep blue eyes, stares at her. "Not like Mother?"

"Mother," Anna says, sitting next to Magda to tie her bonnet back on, "was raised in a city. Very different from the life she chose to have with Father. With us."

"Do you think she regrets leaving?" Magda asks.

"No. City, town, or forest—nothing could have saved anyone from this war." Anna kisses her sister on the cheek. "And she loves Father dearly."

"She would have to," Magda laughs. "Remember the time..."

Anna leans her head on her sister's shoulder and listens to Magda's voice, picturing every family story in detail.

## KATIE

Katie spends the day in bed with her head pounding. The apartment is empty. Both Sam and Carly are at work. Katie groans when she sees the stacks of mail next to her bed. Piles of advertisements mixed in with past-due reminders topple into each other. She doesn't want to look at those. Her checking account hasn't been balanced in over in a month. Intuitively, she knows the money will run out in six. Sooner, if she keeps going to bars and clubs. Tears run down her face. *I have to pull myself together,* she tells herself. But the tears gain momentum until her whole body shakes with loss. Loud and ugly cries fill the room. Katie can't hide anymore.

# ANNA

**Summer 1942, Central Asia**

The train whistles and pulls into a station. Anna thinks they must be near Uzbekistan. She hears officers shouting and train cars opening for inspection. The large door to their car slides open, and hard sunlight shines in. The soldier doesn't notice the girls huddled in a corner and moves on to the next car. Anna creeps along the walls, staying in shadow, and peeks out for a view of the depot.

She sees soldiers lining up with their squads and merchants selling fruit while travelers rush to their trains. It's complete chaos: the perfect time to flee.

"Magda, come, now, before the station director arrives to check the cars," Anna calls into the darkness.

Magda steps out, pulling her mud-stained bonnet around her head. Her cheeks are streaked with dirt, and Anna is thankful for this camouflage. Otherwise, Magda's skin is too pale not to be noticed. They slip out of the train car and walk in step with the crowd.

Anna cannot read the station signs written in a curlicue script. She hears what she thinks are Central Asian and Middle Eastern languages along with Russian. With their bonnets pulled down, they walk out of the train station and follow a group of locals pulling carts of goods to sell in town.

Magda stays silent as Anna strains to pick out something she can understand.

"I will go to the port then. The trading here is getting spare," a man pulling a cart of wheat says to another in Russian.

"Yes, there will be more opportunities in Krasnovodsk. But once the Poles gather, you will be back where you started," the other man responds.

"Then I will go to the next evacuation point. I have so much wheat this season, and the Russians are unable to pay market price."

"This will be your last day with us then?" the other man asks.

Anna tunes out the rest of their conversation. She now knows where she and Magda have to go, but is the information current? The young Russian soldier must have given her outdated information. If she only knew where the Polish Army is now, then she could compare it to the map her father made her memorize.

The dirt road opens up to a hot and dusty marketplace filled with tented stalls. Anna scans the merchants and settles on an elderly man selling dates.

"Do you speak Russian?" Anna asks.

"Hungry? It's a long trek over the steppes," he says in halting Russian. He holds up a bag of dates. "What do you have for these?"

Anna feels around in her apron pocket. "I have homegrown tobacco." She pulls out a small burlap bag filled with her home-dried tobacco.

The man beckons her to bring the bag close. He sniffs it. "Strong," he says with a nod. "I will give you half." He starts to scoop dates out.

Anna puts the tobacco back in her pocket. "The full bag of dates."

The man eyes her and glances at Magda, who is staring at the ground.

"Alright," he says, and they exchange goods. "There is a public water station at the end of the market."

"Thank you." Anna takes Magda's hand and leads her back into the crowd. They walk through the market, enjoying the movement and warmth. Drinking their fill, they sit in a shaded corner with their backs to a wall.

"What next?" Magda asks.

"We have to find a train that will take us into Turkmenistan. From there we have to take it on faith that the merchant has current information. We will go to Krasnovodsk."

"Do you think there will be others like us? Children? Girls like me?" She sounds hopeful.

"Well, if the rumors are true and the Soviet Union has formally granted Poles amnesty to leave, then yes."

"You don't believe them?"

Anna sighs. She is tired and hot. "No, I do not believe gossip. And if we were all free to leave, then why are Mother, Father, and Beata not here?"

"Anna," Magda says in a low voice, "that merchant is pointing at us."

Anna looks over at the grain merchant she eavesdropped on earlier. He is nodding at a Russian soldier who turns and walks toward them.

"There's no place to run," Anna says. "Let me talk."

The soldier walks up to them. "Papers."

"We are orphans from the country. Please, we are trying to reach family who have a farm in the south." Anna tries to cover her Polish accent and sound more like a Russian peasant girl.

The soldier hauls Anna up by her arm and grabs Magda by the hand. "Come with me," he says pulling them down two storefronts and opening a door.

Anna and Magda blink in the room's dim light. They are in a small office where a Russian officer is seated at a desk sifting through documents.

"What have you brought me?" the officer asks, looking up from the piles.

"Two runaways. Filthy Poles if you ask me," the soldier says and spits on Anna's shoe.

"Thank you," the officer says and folds his hands. "I will address it from here."

With an angry glare at Anna, the soldier leaves the office.

The officer leans back in his chair. "What am I to do with you two?"

Anna pulls the traveling papers out from her underskirts and hands them to the officer.

"I see," he says after reading them over. "Ander's Army is rendezvousing in Krasnovodsk, if you do not know already. And I have no time for this Polish evacuation that Stalin agreed to." He glances at the papers again and then at Anna. "And I have no time for two Polish runaways."

"If we were to leave this town, then we would be of no trouble to you," Anna suggests.

"Yes," the officer says and hands her papers back. "That

would be best." He pauses. "Be careful not to cross Mikael again, though. He likes to take matters into his own hands." The officer picks up his pen.

"Thank you," Anna whispers and pulls Magda out of the office back into the glaring sun.

# 37

# KATIE

Katie surveys the boxes filling the living room and kitchen. She squeezes around them and fixes herself a bowl of cereal. Last week, Carly and her fiancé moved into a condo a few towns over, but she has a few remaining boxes to place in storage—along with all of Sam's stuff.

"You coming to help?" Sam calls from her bedroom.

"Coming." Katie finishes her cereal and walks into Sam's room. Clothes are stacked everywhere. "I don't know where to start."

Sam gestures to her bed. "You sit there and put everything I toss you into the donation bags." She turns back to her massive walk-in closet. "This feels right, you know? Purging before the next chapter, doing something good with my life."

Katie slumps on Sam's bed. "But you're a nurse, you do good every day."

"Kind of. But this program is for real, Katie. I'm going to be stationed in a poor village where families are struggling.

Do you know the sort of impact this will have for the girls there? Traditionally, they get married in their teens."

"But is it safe?" Katie is worried.

"Probably as safe as my partying lifestyle here." Sam plunks another pile of clothes for donation on the bed and sits next to Katie. "I'm going to miss you like crazy."

"I know," Katie says and squeezes Sam in a tight hug. "Don't drink any water that isn't boiled."

"Who do you think you're talking to?" Sam questions and goes back to sorting. "It's only for a year. Then, who knows?"

"Yeah, who knows." Katie pushes the pile of clothes into a bag and sets it by the door. "Into the car with the others?"

"Yep, but I have one more." Sam stuffs tight skirts and a pair of thigh-high boots into a bag, then hands it over. "It'll all work out. That's what Babchi always said."

"Yeah, she did," Katie says, smiling at the memory.

38
_____

# ANNA

Hiding in a corner of the train station, Anna watches people board and calculates the ratio of passengers to soldiers. She wonders which of the two trains heading south will be safest.

"Stay here," she tells Magda. "And if I don't come back, you get on that train."

"What do you mean? Alone?"

"If I'm detained, I will find you. Just stay with the Polish Army. Get documented. And remember you are ten."

Magda nods.

Anna smooths down her skirts and walks up and down the length of the train. She spots two young Polish men at the end of the train, smoking and chatting.

"*Dzień dobry*," Anna says.

The two boys turn and smile. "*Dzień dobry*," they say in unison.

There are less people standing around this end of the train, but Anna positions herself behind a column to stay hidden from the main platform.

"Are you evacuating, too?" the blond boy asks.

"Yes, I'm on my way to Turkmenistan," Anna says and offers each of the boys a cigarette.

"Then we should travel together," the other boy with dark brown hair says. He lights the cigarette Anna offers. "We have papers. Do you?" A look of concern crosses his face. "I don't know what will happen if you are undocumented."

The blond boy snorts. "Forgive Jan. He was sheltered by a distant relative and hasn't seen the countryside."

"I have papers," Anna says. "I just have to collect my things."

"Surely, surely," the blond boy says, smiling.

Anna walks away, weighing the advantages of traveling with two Polish boys.

"You're back," Magda says and throws her arms around Anna.

"Stop." Anna pulls free. "Don't attract attention."

"I wouldn't worry about that," Magda says, as two NKVD lead Jan and his blond friend away from the train.

"But we have papers," Jan's voice rises above the din.

"Are they Polish?" Magda asks excitedly.

Anna nods. "Now's our chance."

She grabs Magda's hand and drags her to the middle of the train. On her scouting trip, she picked a non-passenger car filled with wool. As she pushes Magda into the car, she hears two gunshots.

"Quickly, get behind that," Anna says and pushes her sister toward large blocks of wool.

"Anna," Magda quivers, "I'm—"

Anna rushes to Magda and pulls her down. "I know, I know," she says, cradling her sister against her shoulder.

Their backs press into the rough squares. "We will be safe, *kochana*, soon we will be safe."

The door to their car slides shut amid shouts and the roar of the train's engine. The train leaves the depot, and Anna prays that they will find Ander's Army at the end.

**39**

---

## KATIE

Katie packs the last of her dishes in the kitchen, tapes the box shut, and moves it into the living room. She looks around. One more car trip should get the last of her things out of the apartment. Luckily Babchi's house is close.

Katie wanders through the halls, triple-checking that they haven't left anything behind. The rooms are bare. She pauses in the large living and dining area, which is deceivingly void of life. But it still holds all of Katie's shared moments: the beginnings and more endings than she thought she could handle. She pictures Babchi at the dining room table laughing as Sam acted out her most recent drunken adventures. Or Carly red-eyed and weeping when she thought Greg was going to break up with her. Or just last week, when the roommates had their final goodbye dinner with an extra place set for Babchi.

It is the end of a chapter. *But,* Katie thinks as she heaves another box down to her car, *I'm ready for the next.*

# 40

## ANNA

After the train doors close, they do not open again until Turkmenistan. The depot is bustling in a way that reminds Anna of the time before the war. The sisters step out of the car and scan for the NKVD.

"This way, this way." A Russian soldier is waving groups of people out the side of the depot. "Continue down to the port. All Poles continue down to the port."

Anna feels Magda's hand relax in hers.

"Are we here?" she asks. "Is this Krasnovodsk?"

Anna watches as families of thin, unwashed Poles stream down the road. She's happy to see some of the Polish men looking healthy and strong in their new uniforms.

"Yes, *kochana,* we are here." Anna pulls Magda with her to join the line down to the docks.

The mass of people moves steadily. Many of the Poles are subdued, shuffling one foot in front of the other to reach the giant, rusted cargo ships waiting for them on the edge of the Caspian Sea.

Starved Poles peer over the railings as Anna and Magda move forward to the check-in.

"Papers?" a man asks. His makeshift desk is a plank balanced on two barrels. Red Cross workers rush from passenger to passenger, trying to help the worst-off before they board.

Anna hands the man her traveling papers. He raises an eyebrow and shakes his head.

"These are for a man named Bogdan who I'm guessing is a relative, yes?" He nods, not waiting for a response, and moves his hand to an empty line of his ledger. "Name, age, and place of birth for each of you."

Anna breathes in deeply and pulls Magda close to her side. "My name is Anna."

As she rattles off her and her sister's personal information, she thinks soon, soon they will be free from their captors. Afterward, the man ushers them to board the ship, and Anna looks back at the distance between her and her family as she and Magda move farther away from home.

# 41

## KATIE

Katie carries the last box through the front door and into the small living room. *I'll have to get this old carpet ripped up,* she thinks. After carrying the box to her bedroom, she stacks it on Babchi's bureau that she asked her mother to leave. She unpacks the boxes, placing everything carefully into drawers. The scent of violets wafts up, and she wonders if her clothes will smell forever like Babchi's favorite perfume.

Her phone jingles, and she glances at the message. It's Harry, the director at her new library, letting her know that two of the public computers are down. He wants her to take care of it as soon as she gets in. Katie texts back an affirmative. She likes being the sole librarian in the small library. Everyday it's a different challenge, a different task. And she is leading a monthly book group where she's met a few potential friends.

She scrolls down the ongoing list of needed house repairs written out on her phone. There are fifty items so far. The larger renovations will have to wait until her paychecks start accumulating. She walks into the cramped, musty bathroom where early morning sunlight pours in. Babchi must have known Katie would love the house. The foundation is sound, but the interior could use some work. *Just like me,* Katie thinks, patting the old bathroom tiles. She silently thanks Babchi for this gift. This comfort.

Breaking out of her reverie, she closes her list of repair work and looks up contractors and renovators in her area. *Patience,* she reminds herself while scanning countless reviews. *The right person for the job will show up.*

42
___

# ANNA

**Iran**

Anna never saw anything like the parade in Tehran that welcomes the Polish Army. Flowers are strewn everywhere, and there is food and water, as much as they can eat and drink. To Anna, it is paradise.

Magda begins classes with other displaced Polish children in the makeshift school run by the British Army. Anna is deemed too old for school and is trained as a decoder. She spends her days running through enemy ciphers and her evenings flirting with Polish soldiers.

The British government's unspoken condition for the Poles' freedom in Ander's Army is that evacuees not to speak of their mistreatment by the Soviets and Stalin's hand. The Allies needed Stalin to help win the war, and now is not the time for truth.

Soon the Polish Army will move onto Palestine alongside their British allies. Anna is grateful for the luck she and Magda had while traveling. Word came through that the

Russians stopped allowing Poles to evacuate. Her family and countless others are trapped.

Music interrupts Anna's thoughts.

"How can you ignore that one?" Magda asks, pointing to a brown-haired soldier smiling at the sisters.

"Mmm, this is your first dance. Better to be picky," Anna says and turns away from the man's bright eyes.

"Not handsome enough?" Magda laughs.

"We will have to wait and see," Anna says. "I want to keep my options open."

This war may end, Anna believes. And there is a whole world waiting for her.

## KATIE

Katie turns her head at the sound of a knock on the screen door. She pauses, puts down the glass she was washing, and waves at the man standing outside. He is tall and dark-haired; Katie is surprised that the contractor her friend recommended is so handsome.

"Hi," Katie says, wiping her hands dry on her pants and opening the door. "Alberto?"

"Yes, nice to meet you," he says in a thick Brazilian accent and shakes her hand.

Katie ushers him in.

"So, I have a limited budget, but the bathroom is a priority, and the kitchen second."

"Let's see," he says, following Katie through the house.

He looks the bathroom over, and Katie tries not to stare.

"We'll have to replace the drywall and put in new tiles. There's some water damage."

"Wait until you see the kitchen floor. That's where my grandmother left a bag of potatoes to rot. I bet you've never seen anything like it," Katie warns.

He laughs. "I have a ninety-year-old granny who lives in

the countryside all by herself. I don't think much will shock me."

Katie smiles and shows him the kitchen while they swap grandmother stories.

"Let me measure the whole floor," he says and takes out his tape measure.

Katie leans against the doorway jamb to watch him work. She hears Babchi's teasing voice in her head: *This is going to be messy, Katie. But remember, that is living,* moja kochana. *This is life.*

DECADES AGO, sometime in the 1980s, in a small house, a forty-something woman holds a baby girl in her arms. Born prematurely, the tiny infant loves being swaddled from head to toe. Anna rocks her gently and coos softly in Polish. Katie's mother sleeps soundly in the main bedroom. The child calms with Anna's touch, her eyes big and brown. Anna places the baby on the bed and unwraps her for a diaper change. After wiping her clean, she laughs and kisses the baby's toes and blows raspberries on her belly. The baby giggles and gazes up into Anna's eyes.

"*Moja kochana.* My little angel. My Katya."

The child grasps Anna's hand and holds tight.

*Home.*

# AUTHOR'S NOTE

This work was inspired by the experience of my grandmother, or as we called her, Babchi. During WWII she and her family were taken from their home in Poland and deported to a labor camp in Siberia run under Stalin's Soviet Union. Some events described in the book are real, like her dog being shot, as well as, being locked up for days on a cattle car train. While in the labor camp my grandmother and her family starved, resorting to eating grass at one point. Later, as an old woman, she would hoard tinned food and could not sleep if the pantry were empty. We joked if an invading army came again, the soldiers would not allow her to take the food. She would laugh and agree that the mind is a mysterious thing. Then she'd go right back to cutting coupons for more tinned food.

It is unclear how many of her siblings died in Siberia. When reminiscing, my Babchi would sometimes slip and a new piece of information about younger brothers would come out, but then she would shut down again. No one in the family is certain how many siblings she lost due to the labor camp conditions. It was as if speaking or remembering the entirety of her past during the war would be too much to relive. We do know that her father died in Siberia, probably from pneumonia, and her mother, older sister, and brother survived.

As with Anna in the book, my Babchi escaped with her younger sister and joined Ander's Army, but again she did not share the details of the escape other than that they were very lucky. In real life, she and her sister were detained twice while stealing rides on trains. One time, Babchi began to tell me the story of being detained by a Russian officer, but stopped abruptly only offering the words, "It is a miracle we escaped alive." In hindsight, she realized how young and stupid she had been. However, without that recklessness, she said she never would have left the labor camp. In old age she understood that her escape with her sister was dangerous with low odds of survival. Her younger self was impatient, impetuous, and daring. Babchi came to view that reckless naivete as a gift, knowing if she had been more mature and less desperate, she never would have attempted such an audacious feat. Snug in her house in America, she laughed off her youthful indiscretion which allowed her and her sister to find a freedom her family left behind never experienced.

Babchi loved to share how the people of Tehran welcomed the Polish Army, even throwing them a parade. She and her sister thought it was paradise after such brutal cold and hunger. While with the Polish Army, my grandmother trained as a decoder and worked alongside the British. She was at the Battle of Monte Cassino. Then after the war, unable to return to her country that had been annexed to the Soviet Union, she and her husband, were sent to a refugee camp in England. She was cut off from her family in Poland and had no idea who was left alive. Her younger sister fell in love with an Englishman and they married, had children, and a long life together. My Babchi and her husband won a spot through the American lottery system and were sponsored to come to the United States where my grandfather worked in a textile mill until retirement.

Babchi tried not to dwell on the past and was always moving forward. She adored the vastness and beauty of America, traveling to as many National Parks as possible. Later when she was too sick to leave her house, she would watch nature and travel shows. Babchi was proud to have taken American citizenship and worked to be a part of her new country, including voting in every election from local school boards to the presidency. She only went back to Poland once to see her mother and sister. I was young, but remember clearly her anxiety over the visit. Even though she was no longer considered an enemy of the state, she could not trust that her country was safe. Love for her older sister, like Anna had for Beata in the book, overcame Babchi's fear of returning. Years later when her older sister died, Babchi was heartbroken.

As a survivor, Babchi continued to enjoy the little things in life that made her happy: trips to the rose garden, "making" parties for every holiday, and shopping at her favorite store (Kmart). Her younger sister in England visited us in the States once and it was plain to see how attached she was to Babchi. Shortly after hearing of Babchi's death that sister died as well.

I wrote this story out of love: love of a strong, stubborn woman who helped me through my life. It is one of my hopes that the story is a reminder for us to listen to our grandparents' stories, not only to understand where they came from but where we have come from, too. I believe the generational grief experienced by war torn families may be lessened by sharing these stories. Through this sharing perhaps we can help heal our family fears and contribute understanding for other trauma survivors.

~

**A Note for Polish Language Speakers**

The Polish used in the book may not be grammatically "correct" to the native reader. They are simply the Polish words that I heard interspersed with English in my child-hood home.

~

*Baby Anna with her father and mother before the war*

*Anna in the Army after months of care and nourishing
food to eat again*

*Anna and her husband in England*

*Anna and her second child*

*Anna, her husband, and two children*

# ACKNOWLEDGMENTS

I am indebted to all my family and friends who have supported and encouraged me while writing. Most of all thank you to Emily, my best cheerleader and editor.